FOREPLAY TO FURY

Canyon O'Grady turned from the bar as the human mountain named Lash bashed his helpless victim to the floor in one blow. "Out of my way, little man," Lash snarled.

"You're a fool, Lash" Canyon said quietly. "And a bully."

"What was that?" Lash yelled.

"I said, you're a loud-mouthed low-life, is that plain enough?" Canyon said. "Too much of a coward to fight like a man."

The huge man screamed and charged.

And for the first time that night, Canyon grinned.

SIGNET (0451)

JON SHARPE'S WILD WEST

- [ ] **CANYON O'GRADY #1: DEAD MEN'S TRAILS by Jon Sharpe.** Meet Canyon O'Grady, a government special agent whose only badge, as he rides the roughest trails in the West, is the colt in his holster. O'Grady quickly learns that dead men tell no tales, and live killers show no mercy as he hunts down the slayer of the great American hero Merriwether Lewis.
(160681—$2.95)

- [ ] **CANYON O'GRADY #2: SILVER SLAUGHTER by Jon Sharpe.** With a flashing grin and a blazing gun, Canyon O'Grady rides the trail of treachery, greed, and gore in search of nameless thieves who are stealing a vital stream of silver bullion from the U.S. government. (160703—$2.95)

- [ ] **CANYON O'GRADY #3: MACHINE GUN MADNESS by Jon Sharpe.** A gun was invented that spat out bullets faster than a man could blink and every malcontent in the Union wanted it. Canyon's job was to ride the most savage crossfire the West had ever seen to rescue the deadliest weapon the world had ever known. (161521—$2.95)

- [ ] **CANYON O'GRADY #4: SHADOW GUNS by Jon Sharpe.** With America split between North and South and Missouri being a border state both sides wanted, Canyon O'Grady finds himself in a crossfire of doublecross trying to keep a ruthless pro-slavery candidate from using bullets to win a vital election. (162765—$3.50)

- [ ] **CANYON O'GRADY #5: THE LINCOLN ASSIGNMENT by Jon Sharpe.** Bullets, not ballots, were Canyon O'Grady's business as top frontier troubleshooter for the U.S. Government. But now he was tangled up in election intrigue, as he tried to stop a plot aimed at keeping Abe Lincoln out of office by putting him in his grave. (163680—$3.50)

- [ ] **CANYON O'GRADY #6: COMSTOCK CRAZY by Jon Sharpe.** Canyon O'Grady hits a murder-mad town with blazing guns as he rides into Virginia City with an impossible clean-up job to do, an unspeakable slaying to avenge, and an unbeatable trigger finger itching for rapid-fire action.
(164423—$3.50)

- [ ] **CANYON O'GRADY #7: THE KING OF COLORADO by Jon Sharpe.** A great new Western hero in a battle royal against a reign of terror, Canyon O'Grady is up against the maddest, most murderous threat ever to ravish the Wild West ... (165470—$3.50)

Buy them at your local bookstore or use this convenient coupon for ordering.
NEW AMERICAN LIBRARY
P.O. Box 999, Bergenfield, New Jersey 07621

Please send me the books I have checked above. I am enclosing $_____ (please add $1.00 to this order to cover postage and handling). Send check or money order—no cash or C.O.D.'s. Prices and numbers are subject to change without notice.

Name_____

Address_____

City _____ State _____ Zip _____

Allow 4-6 weeks for delivery.
This offer, prices and numbers are subject to change without notice.

9

COUNTERFEIT MADAM

by
Jon Sharpe

A SIGNET BOOK

SIGNET
Published by the Penguin Group
Penguin Books USA Inc., 375 Hudson Street, New York,
New York 10014, U.S.A.
Penguin Books Ltd, 27 Wrights Lane, London W8 5TZ, England
Penguin Books Australia Ltd, Ringwood, Victoria, Australia
Penguin Books Canada Ltd, 2801 John Street, Markham, Ontario,
Canada L3R 1B4
Penguin Books (N.Z.) Ltd, 182-190 Wairau Road, Auckland 10, New Zealand

Penguin Books Ltd, Registered Offices: Harmondsworth, Middlesex, England

First published by Signet, an imprint of New American Library, a division of Penguin Books USA Inc.

First Printing, September, 1990
10 9 8 7 6 5 4 3 2 1

Copyright © Jon Sharpe, 1990
All rights reserved
The first chapter of this book appeared in *Bleeding Kansas*, the eighth volume in this series.

 REGISTERED TRADEMARK—MARCA REGISTRADA

Printed in the United States of America

Without limiting the rights under copyright reserved above, no part of this publication may be reproduced, stored in or introduced into a retrieval system or transmitted, in any form, or by any means (electronic, mechanical, photocopying, recording, or otherwise), without prior written permission of both the copyright owner and the above publisher of this book.

PUBLISHER'S NOTE
This is a work of fiction. Names, characters, places, and incidents either are the product of the author's imagination or are used fictitiously, and any resemblance to actual persons, living or dead, events, or locales is entirely coincidental.

BOOKS ARE AVAILABLE AT QUANTITY DISCOUNTS WHEN USED TO PROMOTE PRODUCTS OR SERVICES. FOR INFORMATION PLEASE WRITE TO PREMIUM MARKETING DIVISION, PENGUIN BOOKS USA INC., 375 HUDSON STREET, NEW YORK, NEW YORK 10014.

Canyon O'Grady

His was a heritage of blackguards and poets, fighters and lovers, men who could draw a pistol and bed a lass with the same ease.

Freedom was a cry seared into Canyon O'Grady, justice a banner of his heart.

With the great wave of those who fled to America, the new land of hope and heartbreak, solace and savagery, he came to ride the untamed wildness of the Old West.

With a smile or a six-gun, Canyon O'Grady became a name feared by some and welcomed by others, but remembered by all. . . .

August, 1860 in eastern Minnesota, where a trail of deception led through a forest of betrayal and avarice . . .

1

Canyon O'Grady had seen enough bodies to know that Rufus J. Thorndike had been dead at least six hours. The small, bald man had been shot twice in the chest so close that the powder burns showed. He probably died instantly from the one round through his heart. A small desk to one side of his office had been thoroughly searched, quickly, messily, and probably unsuccessfully. Papers were scattered, and the pigeonholes in the front of the rolltop had been emptied and dumped on the desk.

Robbery hadn't been the motive. Several stock certificates lay on the floor. Obviously, the killer was looking for the same thing as O'Grady.

A pad of paper half-covered by the mess on the desk showed a string of small pictures, basic sketches anyone might make. O'Grady looked at them again. They formed a pictograph. The first showed a fish, then a falls. Next came a half-moon with stars around it, and a small boat and two stick figures. Rufus must have hoped that he and another man could go fishing one night at the falls in a two-man boat.

But that wasn't much help in O'Grady's search. He found three more of the picture messages, one describing a night of love and passion with a woman with long dark hair. He skipped the others and kept looking for a clue. A small file drawer in the desk produced nothing helpful.

O'Grady sat in the dead man's desk chair and rocked back. Where would I hide information if I was scared? Sure, I'd hide it in my brain, but where else? O'Grady powered his imagination into high gear for a pretending game.

Where? How? In the office, at the desk probably, but how? He looked back at the two pictographs he had skipped. No luck.

Squares of paper had been tacked in a row along the wall beside the desk. A handwritten message on one of the papers reminded Rufus that he needed to go to the dentist on Tuesday. He wouldn't make it. Another note in ink had a date and a time, three days hence at 7:30 P.M. One showed a nonartistic sketch of the head and shoulders of the dark-haired woman. A date perhaps?

O'Grady stood and paced the room. He was looking at things the wrong way. He went as far from the desk and note wall as he could get and stared at them. Small notes were everywhere. Thorndike had been a visually activated man. If he could see a note, he wouldn't forget the event.

O'Grady looked back at the row of papers. There were various colors of paper used. He hadn't picked up on that before. The man wrote everything important on paper.

Now O'Grady looked at the various colors of paper. There was a rough line of light-blue paper, with a half-dozen five-by-seven-inch sheets tacked to the wall. But there were other notes and colors interspersed. He studied only the blue pages.

Taking them in order meant nothing: a lodge meeting, an appointment with the banker, a note to call the pastor before church Sunday, a figure of $20, a list of food to buy. The last one was a fishing date for Saturday.

Canyon tried switching the order. Still nothing had anything to do with money except the twenty dollars. Not good enough. He went back to the far wall and looked again. He found five notes on soft red paper on the wall, again with other colors of paper in between.

The red papers made up a strange collection: one sketch showed a river falls, another a building with lumber around it, the third was ten lines drawn in two sets of five with the fifth and tenth lines crossing the other four. The next-to-last red sheet had a drawing of a kerosene lamp with red rays of a crayon coming from it. The last red sheet showed nothing but a sun peeking over the horizon, and two arrows.

O'Grady felt a tingle. This was it, this was what Rufus would have told him if he had lived. Quickly now, O'Grady went to the wall and removed the five sheets of red paper, folded them, and put them securely in his inside jacket pocket. Then he walked out of the office, closed the door, and stepped into the lumber town called Minneapolis, Minnesota.

He walked two blocks to the Minnesota River. Considering the sketches in order, Canyon recalled there was a falls nearby, on Minnehaha Creek.

But there were other falls around as well. They

provided power for the grain mills and the lumber mills that were Minneapolis's life. So he had the falls and the sawmills. What did the ten marks mean?

The lamp with the red rays meant nothing to O'Grady either. Was it a rising or setting sun? What did the arrows mean? One went up toward the top of the page, the other pointed to the right. There were no obvious answers.

O'Grady walked along A Street and saw a large sawmill, pond, and stacks of drying lumber to the north. He walked to the south, downstream on the river, and soon saw another mill. Both used the river falls for power. But they weren't ten miles from town or each other. He was stumped.

Canyon O'Grady wandered north to the business section and turned down Main Street. In a small café just this side of Minnesota Street he ordered a cup of coffee. He spread out the sheets of paper and studied them again.

When the young waitress brought his coffee, she looked at the papers with surprise. "Do you like picture puzzles, too? I just love them. Mr. Thorndike likes to play games that way. He comes in once in a while and he gives me a pictograph for his order. Once, as a joke, I brought him a whole uncooked chicken on a plate."

She was maybe eighteen, open, friendly, not jaded yet.

"He come in here often?"

"He used to; then a couple of weeks ago, he said he was going to stay indoors. He thought somebody was following him. Haven't seen him now in a while. You know what that picture puzzle says?"

"No. A friend gave it to me and I'm stumped. A waterfall, a sawmill, ten of something, a lamp, and a sunrise maybe because one arrow points upward. I don't know about the other arrow."

"Mmmmmmmm. Let me see. Sometimes Mr. Thorndike would put them on different pieces of paper this way and mix up the order so it would be harder to figure. That might be the same here. Let's see. It's something about a sawmill at a river falls, that's for sure. 'Course we got falls and rivers and sawmills all over the place, even all the way to the St. Croix River over to the east edge of the state."

The girl grinned. "Well, that could be. You take the sunrise picture and put it first, then the river, the falls, and the sawmill. Biggest sawmill operations to the east of us is all the way out to Stillwater on the St. Croix. There's a falls there that powers lots of sawmills."

"You think it might refer to Stillwater, rather than a Minneapolis sawmill?

"Oh, yeah. Why else put in the sunrise and the arrows to the east? See, on a map the top is always north and the bottom south, so when you face north, east is on your right. And the sun rises in the east. Yep, I definitely think that's the first part of the picture puzzle. Them other two don't give me no ideas at all."

The waitress grinned. "You want anything else, a doughnut maybe or a piece of home-baked cherry pie?"

"I'll try the pie."

Her smile brightened the café. "Good! You'll like it. Made it myself." She leaned close to look at the sketches again. "Lordy, I just can't figure out that ten or the lamp. Stillwater is maybe twenty miles over east. I'll fetch that pie."

When she brought back the pie, she propped her chin in her hands and studied the five pictures again. She shook her head.

"Glory, I just can't figure it. They don't go together easy like most of them I see. Is it important?"

"Friendly little bet. I could lose five dollars."

"In that case, I'll think on it. The lamp with the red beams tickles my fancy, but I can't quite remember what it means or where it is. I might. You stop by for supper."

O'Grady finished the pie and coffee, waved to the waitress, and ambled down the street. He walked into the county sheriff's office in the rough-hewn wood-frame courthouse and found the man in. He had two assistants and three deputies in the office. O'Grady persuaded one of the deputies he needed to see the boss.

His name was Sheriff Longtree and he wasn't smiling.

"I'm busy today, just found a man shot in his own office. Terrible. No clues, but some powder burns. What's your complaint?"

"No complaint, Sheriff. More like a puzzle. Trying to find a friend of mine, and all he left me were these five drawings." O'Grady spread them out on the lawman's desk.

"Hell, I don't have time to play games. You might talk to Melvin out front. He plays with pictographs sometimes. Used to drive me crazy with them."

O'Grady found Melvin. The deputy's eyes sparkled when he saw the drawings.

"Love these things. Any order to 'em?"

O'Grady shook his head.

Melvin studied them. "The obvious are easy, but what is the ten for, and the sunrise?" He looked at the lamp and the red rays. "I've never seen one in color before, those red rays. Yeah, there is one place nearby that the sheriff tells me the whores are hanging red lamps in their windows when they're looking for customers. A kind of ready-for-you sign. Sheriff says he's calling it a red-light house. Think that's important?"

"Could be," O'Grady said. "Just where is this place with the red lights?"

"Oh, not in Minneapolis. It's in Stillwater, eighteen, twenty miles to the east."

O'Grady nodded. Stillwater had to be his next stop. He let Melvin play with the pictures for awhile, then O'Grady shuffled them together.

"Thanks a lot. Maybe I'll get a sudden inspiration over a tall glass of whiskey."

The stage office didn't have any trips to Stillwater until the next noon. O'Grady didn't want to wait that long. He wished he had Cormac there, but the big palomino stallion with the pale-bronze coat and white tail and mane was resting somewhere outside of Denver. There had been no time to get him to Minnesota.

At the hotel, O'Grady packed what little he had taken out of his carpetbag and walked to the livery, where he hired a horse and saddle. A half-hour later he was on his way to Stillwater. He wasn't sure what he would find when he got there, but at least he had some clues. He should arrive in the town on the St. Croix River sometime around eight that evening.

The blood bay he had chosen from the livery was lively enough and deep-chested, so O'Grady let her out a little now and then to see what she could do. He hadn't brought anything to eat, so the cherry pie had to last him until he got into the sawmill hamlet. The livery man had said Stillwater had not more than a thousand souls in it even if you counted the goats.

It was eight-thirty and dark when he rode down the muddy street and checked out the buildings of Stillwater. They were all made of rough-sawn lumber from the nearby lumber mills; it looked like the whole town could burn down in about thirty seconds.

There were the usual general stores and saloons, a hardware store, and a tinsmith. O'Grady passed one hotel that had been built just slightly off square.

He chose another hotel four doors down, The Lumberman's Hotel, which had only two stories and a small restaurant he spotted past the lobby. The U.S. agent registered, ate a mediocre meal, then stashed his gear in Room 24 on the second floor front.

The smell of wood smoke was everywhere. He guessed not a shovelful of coal was ever burned in this town. They had plenty of bark and edges and slab wood as well as the ends off the trim saw to fire five hundred wood stoves and fireplaces.

It was nine-thirty now, and O'Grady felt it might be a good time to check in at the local gossip mill. He headed for Aces High, the biggest saloon in town.

It was across the street and two doors down from his hotel. Inside, he saw what he expected.

Aces High was a gambling-drinking-whoring saloon, with a fancy staircase that led along one wall to the second floor, where he guessed there were a dozen cribs for handy use. The girls didn't pose prettily in some salon upstairs. Instead, they worked the tables, serving drinks and having their bottoms pinched.

It was a rugged kind of saloon, not given to fancy mirrors or expensive furniture. The plank floor was chewed up with the tracks of hobnail boots used by loggers and pond men. Sturdy wooden chairs bellied up to square solid tables. Drunks didn't smash through a table here; instead, they bounced off and hit the floor.

O'Grady went to the bar and bought a mug of beer for a dime and sat at the side of the saloon with his back to the wall. As he sipped the beer, he watched and listened.

The talk was all logging and lumbering, felling trees, and sawing them into boards.

A slender dance-hall girl leaned over his table and stared. "You're new in town. I'd never miss that red hair. It's hot enough to start a fire. See anything you like?"

As she leaned over, the bodice of the low-cut dress billowed out and allowed a clear view down to her navel. Her breasts were firm and just the right size to be cupped by a man's hand.

She let him have a good look, then sat down across from him. "Make you happy for just a lousy two dollars," she said. "I'm Patsy."

"Patsy, I'm not buying, but I'll set you up to a watered whiskey and we can talk."

"Beer, I'm a beer drinker." She went to the bar and came back with one for herself and a fresh one for him. She pocketed the quarter he gave her and tipped the beer. "So, what do we talk about?"

"Ten," he said.

"Pardon me?"

"Ten. Does that number mean anything special here in town?"

"Ten what?"

"That's what I don't know. An old friend gave me a puzzle to figure out. I can't figure what the ten stands for."

"Hey, you're looking for a brain, lumberjack. I just sell a body. You want to buy it tonight or not?"

"I'm broke, sweetheart. But if you don't need the two bucks, I'll be glad to run upstairs."

Patsy snorted, then grinned. "Hell, I'm half-tempted to do it." She traced a finger around his jawline. "I ain't seen a handsome bunch of man like you in this dump in a long time." She stood, pulled in a deep breath, and slowly shook her head. "Truth is, I can't afford it, and I'd get my ass whacked good and proper for wasting my time and not making any cash money for the bastard who pushes us. Try me again when I'm a little bit drunk." She took the beer and hurried over toward a table where two young men had just arrived.

"Young feller, could I bother you for the use of a chair?"

O'Grady looked up at the older man who stood beside the table. He was well into his sixties and held two mugs of beer, one in each hand. He winked one green eye.

"Hell, what I really wanted was to sit down and talk. All I do anymore is talk. You busy, stranger? I sure ain't seen you around town before."

O'Grady motioned to the chair. "Sit, rest yourself. You can fill me in on the local politics, how the wind is blowing and where the bodies are buried. You up to all that?"

"On only two beers?" the old-timer asked. His odd laugh sailed into the loftier ranges.

"That won't be a problem," O'Grady said. "This looks like a sawmill town, pure and simple."

"Hell, if it ain't. Oh, my manners. Name's Ira. Yep, we chop and drag and saw. Do a lot of floating, too."

"How many mills here?"

"Two that 'mount to anything. Biggest is the Rombold Lumber Company. Three Rombold brothers run the place. They ain't the woodsmen their father was. He started the outfit. Rombold drags a lot of weight hereabouts. Employ more than half the timber workers in town."

"The other one is smaller?"

"By about four times. It's the Norgard Sawmilling and Lumber Company. I've worked for both of them. Still on the Norgard payroll. It's the class of the pair. But somebody wants both of them out of business. Big fire last night did a lot of damage. And another one hit Rombold later on."

Ira tipped the mug of beer he'd been working on. His brown eyes looked up and locked on O'Grady. "So, you're out of questions already?"

19

"How is the law here?"

"Sheriff Spurlock is a good man. I'd trust him at my back in a shoot-out."

"Does the number ten have any special meaning in Stillwater?" O'Grady asked.

"Ten? Ten what? Ten pennies in a dime? Ten dimes in a dollar?"

"I don't know. Friend of mine gave me a puzzle to figure out, and ten is part of it."

Ira shook his head. His white hair sailed from side to side and came to a rest only when he stopped. "Nope, no such thing as an important 'ten' in Stillwater. I been here for thirty years, I should know."

"Then you must know all the best whores in town."

"Darn tootin'!"

"What's the biggest whorehouse in town now?" O'Grady asked.

"Charity House. Charity is the madam. Runs a nice clean place."

They talked for a half-hour more. O'Grady bought the old man another beer and headed outside. Across the street a man and a woman stepped gingerly off the boardwalk into the muddy street. A buggy rolled down the street toward them.

In a moment there was a gunshot, and the horse screamed and darted forward, jerking the reins out of the startled driver's hands. The horse bolted ahead in panic, a runaway.

The rig headed directly at the man and woman in midstreet. The man lunged forward to save her, but he slipped and fell on his stomach in the street. The woman rushed ahead six steps, looked at the rampaging horse, and froze in panic.

O'Grady darted into the muddy street and charged toward the woman, who didn't seem able to move. Her companion struggled to his feet, then slipped again.

O'Grady raced forward, hoping he could get to the woman before the horse ran her down. He had another ten feet to go. It would be close. . . .

2

Canyon O'Grady wasn't nervous about this evening in Washington, D.C. General Wheeler had told him to dress formally and attend the presidential ball in the Executive Mansion. Sometime during the dancing, he would be directed to a nearby room to talk with President James Buchanan.

O'Grady had long ago reached the point in his self-confidence so that powerful figures, famous people, or deadly criminals generated no awe in him, held no fear and no jealousy. All of these people were simply men or women, and he was able to hold his head up with any of them.

He wore the prescribed black frock coat, a ruffled-front white shirt with a white winged stock tie. His black trousers had a thin stripe of black ribbon down each side.

O'Grady had been in this ballroom before, but not with this much of a crush of humanity. He found the punch bowl and sipped at the spiced fruit punch as he watched the people. At first he saw no one he knew, then here and there a face appeared that he recognized. He spotted Philip Thomas, the secretary of the treasury. A few moments later Jeremiah Black, the president's secretary of state danced by.

Canyon had just moved away from the punch bowl when someone spoke behind him.

"Mr. O'Grady, I need to talk to you for a moment."

The U.S. agent turned around and saw General Wheeler in his civilian clothes. He stood ramrod-straight and there was no mistaking him for anything other than a military man.

"General Wheeler, of course. I've been looking for you."

O'Grady followed the general through a door at the far side of the ballroom, down a hall and into another hallway, then Wheeler turned again and entered a room with a large desk. It was not the president's usual office. The formal trappings of state were not here. It looked more like a place where the president could get some work done.

President Buchanan sat behind the cherrywood desk. Another man in formal wear stood to his left. On the desktop were four neatly arranged stacks of papers. He wrote on a pad with a pencil for a moment, then looked up. "Ah, yes, Agent O'Grady. It seems we have another problem that hasn't been solved, so we call on you again."

"Thank you, Mr. President."

"Wait until you find out what the problem is before you thank me, son," the white-haired man said. He stared at O'Grady for just a moment from deep-set eyes hiding under pure-white bushy brows. There was a tiredness in the man's face that was easy to see. O'Grady knew that the president was nearly seventy and that the slavery-antislavery question had been giving him much more trouble than he had expected it would.

He looked up. "Well, we better get to it." He motioned to the other man. "I would expect that you know the Secretary of the Treasury Philip Thomas. He'll give you the gist of the matter."

Thomas stepped forward and handed O'Grady a sheet of paper from one of the stacks on the desk. It was hundred-dollar United States treasury bond.

"Have you seen these before, Mr. O'Grady?"

"No, sir. I don't have many investments."

"A good thing you didn't buy this one. It's a forgery, a counterfeit, worthless outside of its value as a piece of art."

O'Grady waited.

"So far we have discovered two of these, both in the same city. They are excellent copies, beautifully engraved and printed. However, these bonds all have identical numbers on them. Real ones are numbered individually, consecutively."

O'Grady inspected the certificate again.

"Frankly, it's damn good work," the secretary continued. "It took one of our experts to pick this forgery out when we covered up the serial numbers on all the bonds. We sent two treasury department field men to Minneapolis, and in two weeks they came up with almost nothing. Thorndike, the broker who turned these two in to us, was of little help. He had bought them with some other stocks and bonds when one of his older clients died and the widow asked him to liquidate them and bring her cash.

"Thorndike is still in Minneapolis, and he will

give you all the help he can. Our investigators came up empty and we thought it prudent to recall them and send in someone new. That's why you are here."

"Mr. Secretary, I know little about stocks and bonds."

"We know that, O'Grady," President Buchanan said softly. "You were my choice. We don't need a professional detective on this one. We need a man who can do some snooping and get into the rough-and-tumble with the locals. Minneapolis is an oversized mill town. Mostly lumber there, although there is more and more wheat coming in for milling.

"I want you to get out there immediately. Look around awhile. Let it be known why you're in town, and see what you can root out. We're not talking any delicate maneuvering here. We need to blast this thing open with some bold moves."

"I understand, Mr. President."

"Your contact name in Minneapolis is Rufus J. Thorndike," the secretary said. "He's a stocks-and-bonds salesman, and he works out of his house near the downtown section of Minneapolis. We have his name and address and the work the other team did in this folder. I'd suggest you don't take along a counterfeit bond. It could be dangerous for you if they know you have that specific bond. Any questions?"

"That's all we know?"

"A little more in the folder, not much. It contains rail tickets as well. We want you there fast."

"How big a problem could this become, the counterfeit bonds?" O'Grady asked.

"Right now, Mr. O'Grady, the federal government has a debt of about sixty-five million dollars. Given a good printing press and a ten- or twelve-state organization for sales, one expert printer with this one engraved plate could turn out and sell ten million dollars' worth of spurious bonds. It could ruin the public trust in our legitimate bonds. It could be a disaster if the government could not sell additional genuine bonds when we need to raise money that does not come by taxation and other revenues. Carried to the extreme it could cause the failure of the federal government and a complete breakdown of law and order in our nation."

"I understand," O'Grady said. "This could be a single forger in a shack in Minneapolis, or it could be a sophisticated printing plant with a hundred salesmen."

"Wish we had more for you O'Grady," President Buchanan said. He looked at Secretary Thomas. "Thanks, Phil. I need to talk to O'Grady for a moment."

The secretary mumbled good-bye and left the room.

"Canyon, I asked you to stay to give you a small present." Buchanan said. "I like to fire a revolver, but I can't abide those linen-wrapped shot and powder lash-ups. I'm pushing for solid round cartridges for our army revolvers the way they have them for the rifles. No damn reason we have to use percussion pistols in this modern era." He handed a revolver across the desk to O'Grady. It had a six-barrel and a cylinder, but no spot for the nipples where the percussion caps were to be placed.

"It's called a *pistolet,* and comes from France.

The best part is that it uses solid cartridges. You'll notice it's a little smaller than the weapon you're used to. It's a .38 caliber, but you can load it in a quarter of the time you'd take to load a percussion revolver."

O'Grady held the weapon and balanced it. Not bad. He liked it. "Mr. President, this is remarkable. I've wished for such an easy-to-load revolver myself more than once. Usually it's just after I fire that fifth round and need three more in a hurry."

The president pushed two boxes across the table. "Here are two hundred rounds, which should last you for a while. I'll order some more from my supplier so you won't run out. I have a *pistolet* just like it and I'm pleased with it." He stood, handed O'Grady the file folder with the material and the train tickets, and nodded. "Good to see you again, O'Grady. I'll be grateful if you can tie up this loose cannon we have rolling around our deck."

"Thank you, Mr. President. I'll do the best I can." He found his way back to the ballroom, and after a while he headed for his hotel room, where he read through the reports on the counterfeiting of U.S. treasury bonds. When he finished, he read everything again. Satisfied, he turned out the light. He had a long train ride ahead.

3

A pair of shadowy figures slipped silently through a two-wire fence and into the Norgard Sawmilling and Lumber Company's drying yard. Ten- and twelve-foot tall stacks of freshly cut boards sat in the flat yard to dry in the Minnesota sunshine. It was well after midnight.

The figures blended into the deep shadows in back of a stack of drying two-by-fours and waited. The guard came past, walking his assigned route. He had half of the yard and the mill to cover, and was by now tired and more than a little sleepy. He carried a shotgun, but he had never used it.

He turned past the stack of lumber and never felt the two-by-four club him on the back of the head. He went down like a square-cut fir tree.

"Drag him back," one voice commanded.

The man who had hit the guard caught him by the shoulders and dragged him almost to the fence and left him.

Quickly the two men toppled the big stacks of lumber. Soon more than a dozen had been tumbled together. A half-dozen sticks of pitch wood placed under the fallen lumber fed a fire that was fanned by a freshening breeze.

The green fir and pine had plenty of pitch in them, and the lumber burned furiously. Soon it lit up the sky.

The two figures slipped away through the fence and well back out of the light of the now-raging inferno. . . .

The next morning, Lon Cumberland sat in his Lumberman's Hotel room on Stillwater's Main Street, and waited. He didn't mind. He'd be a rich man within an hour. Well, not rich exactly, but it was the second huge step in becoming wealthy. He went to the window and pulled down the shade halfway, cutting out most of the sunlight. He sat in one of the darkened room's two wooden chairs with his back to the light.

Yes, the man Lon was waiting for would have to look at him against the glare. No sense in giving away anything he didn't have to, like his identity. Cumberland slouched in the chair, his heavy body overflowing it. He rubbed a meaty, ink-stained hand across his forehead. He shouldn't be sweating. The hard work was done; now the rewards would come, twelve hundred and fifty rewards, Cumberland thought. He laughed softly. His hard brown eyes stared down at the package on the floor, and he reached for it.

A knock on the door interrupted him.

"Come in," Cumberland said with a firm voice of authority.

The man who opened the door was sparse as a

Kansas stalk of corn in October. He held a town hat in his hands and carried a small suitcase. His shoes had been polished once but now showed mud splatters from the street.

"You the supplier?" the man at the door asked. He had taken one step in and held the door open.

"I'm the man you want. Come in and close the door, then turn the key in the lock and leave it there."

The sparse man's lean face frowned slightly; he lifted his heavy brows but did as he was told. He put the suitcase beside the wall. "I come looking to make an investment," the visitor said.

It was the contact phrase to make sure this was the right man.

"I have an investment that can make you rich," Lon Cumberland said, and gave a small sigh of relief after he had replied with the counter phrase.

"Good," the visitor said. "Can we get some light in here so we can see what we're doing?"

"No, sir. I prefer it this way. There's another chair over there. Draw it up and I'll show you the merchandise."

The sparse man frowned again for a moment, shrugged, and drew up the second chair. Instead of sitting in it, he waited for Cumberland, who laid on it a package wrapped in brown paper. It was a bundle eight by twelve inches. On top of the stack was a fancy certificate covered in elaborate scrollwork.

The thin man picked one of the certificates off the stack and carried it to the window, where he studied it for some time. He came back, a smile wreathing his sallow face.

"Indeed, sir, this is good work. I have bought and sold numerous United States treasury bonds. It is virtually impossible to tell this from the genuine article."

"That was my intent, sir," Cumberland said with an icy tone. "I am a professional. You get only the finest workmanship and the right kind of paper, of course. I had to send to Virginia to find it."

"How many?"

"The agreed-upon number of twenty-five, unless you want fifty."

"Twenty-five is fine. The price. I'm willing to go thirty dollars."

Cumberland took the bond from the man's hand at once and put it back on the stack. "The price is fifty dollars, as was arranged. Otherwise this interview is over."

"Hold on, hold on," the thin man said. "Agreed. I was just trying to bargain. Agreed, fifty dollars."

"Please count the bonds," Cumberland said.

The man knelt on the floor beside the chair and counted the heavy sheets of paper that had been so painstakingly engraved and printed. He went through them a second time and nodded. "Yes, twenty-five."

"The payment please, twelve hundred and fifty dollars. You have it in gold, as I requested?"

The sparse man brought out two bags attached at his waist. Cumberland set the soft leather bags on top of the certificates and counted the coins. When he was satisfied, he lifted the bags and stood.

"Needless to say, you are to forget at once where you obtained these bonds. There will be no correspondence. When you have need for twenty-five or fifty more, contact the same lady you did before at the same place, in person, and leave a message."

"Indeed," the other said. He picked up the securely wrapped parcel and put it inside the suitcase near the door. The thin man smiled in the dim light. "Indeed, sir, it is a pleasure to do business with you. I hope to have these sold, and return for more. When will you have more ready?"

"On order."

The man with the suitcase unlocked the door, nodded slightly, and walked out, closing the door gently behind him.

Lon Cumberland ran his hands through his thinning brown hair and looked at the bags of gold on the chair. He had just taken in as much money as the average sawmill worker would make in three years of muscle-tearing labor. He stared at the gold on the chair, then looked out the window at the slice of the rough lumbering town's Main Street that he could see.

A smile billowed around his fleshy face. "Oh, yes," he said softly. The thrill of copying a United States treasury bond exactly was marvelous. But it didn't half-compare to selling twenty-five of the printed masterpieces for such a great sum of money.

The first ten bonds he had placed had been a thrill, but nothing like this. He now had a dealer, an outlet, an agent in the wholesale market, which removed him from the risk and danger and greatly expanded the number of bonds he should be able to pass.

Cumberland stood, pushed the bags of gold inside his white shirt, and let his black business coat cover them. He slipped quietly out of Room 24 and walked rapidly down the corridor to the stairs. He went down the rear steps to the side door and into the cross street a third of a block from Main.

Ten minutes later he slipped into the back door at the Charity House and walked past the kitchen, then along a hallway. One of the doorways opened and a man came out. He didn't look at Lon, just hurried down the hall. Another door opened and a girl wearing only a robe, which was open from neck to toes, watched him.

"Not today, Elmira," he said. She pouted as he passed. He continued to the end of the hall to the last room, which had a painted star on the door. He knocked twice.

"Yeah?" a muted voice came from inside.

Cumberland pushed the door open and stepped into a bedroom.

A plump woman with henna-red hair sat on a fancy padded bench looking into a large mirror, rouging her cheeks. She was dressed, but the buttons down the front of her blouse were open. She saw Cumberland in the mirror and grinned. "How did it go?"

She turned, watching him. She was short, much too heavy and didn't give a damn. Lon's grin gave him away. "He bought them?" she asked. "All of them, at fifty dollars?"

Cumberland closed the door and nodded, his face beaming, his big smile almost squeezing shut his eyes. He drew out the two bags of double eagles and dropped them on the fancy bed with the soft pink bedspread and fluffy cushions.

Charity squealed as she grabbed one of the leather pouches and opened the drawstring. "Celebration time," she said, her voice going low and throaty. "Nothing gets me all sexy like twelve hundred and fifty dollars in gold."

She stood and moved to the bed. She sat down, pushed the blouse off her shoulders, and whipped the silk chemise up and over her head. Her big breasts bounced and jiggled into view. After forty years they sagged a little, but they were large and still firm. She had rouged her areolae and her nipples to a bright pink.

Lon Cumberland growled and caught one of her breasts and pushed her over backward on the bed and fell on top of her.

"I thought the sight of all that gold would get your tits in a whirl. Like you said, it's celebration time, and you and me gonna celebrate until I can't get it hard anymore."

"Right on top of the gold," she whispered. "I want to spread it out and lay on it."

Cumberland laughed. "Why not?" He emptied the gold on the bed and chuckled. "Charity, you and me are a lot alike, you know that? We're both a couple of whores. We both fuck people for money."

Charity nodded. "If you say so, rich man. But I get more fun out of my fucking than you do. All you get is gold."

4

O'Grady pumped his arms as he ran across the dark, muddy street, dashing straight at the frozen woman.

She stared, horrified at the runaway horse and buggy charging directly at her.

Two more steps! O'Grady caught the woman in his arms, lifted her from where she stood, and lunged away from the onrushing horse. They both staggered forward another step, then he held her and dived forward to the street. They rolled away from the horse. The wheel of buggy whacked against O'Grady's boot as it tore past.

He felt the woman lying on top of him. His shoulder ached where he had slammed into the street. For just a moment neither of them moved.

"Oh, my," a woman's soft voice said. "I'm afraid I'm lying here right on you."

By that time two men had rushed up and lifted the woman off O'Grady and then one helped him to his feet.

A third man struggled up, muddy from toe to nose. He must have been the man who had fallen down. He held out his muddy hand. O'Grady shook it with his own muddy hand.

"Sir, I'm Milt Norgard. I'm mighty thankful for your saving the life of my sister. Don't know what would have happened to Felicia if you hadn't charged up and grabbed her. Are you hurt? I'll gladly have your suit cleaned."

O'Grady liked this man. "No broken bones I can find, so far. My name's Canyon O'Grady. Glad I could be some help."

The woman with her muddy jacket and skirt was about five foot three, slender, with long brown hair around her shoulders. Now her cheek had a muddy smudge and the shoulder and front of her pretty blue jacket were mud-smeared. Her glance caught O'Grady's for a moment.

"And I want to thank you. I . . . I don't know what happened. I saw that horse coming and I knew it was a runaway. I took five or six steps and then I couldn't move. It was like my shoes were nailed to the street. All I could do was stare at those big hooves and the powerful chest and legs pounding toward me."

"You're most welcome," O'Grady said. "I just happened to be the one close enough to help." He watched her. He noticed her dimples and a snub nose that gave her face a delightful look all her own.

"Are you sure your shoulder is all right?" Felicia asked. "We hit the ground terribly hard."

"That's what the mud is for," O'Grady said. "It let us skid along and took the sting out of the fall."

"Oh," she said, then smiled. "I've never thought of mud as being a lot of good, but it certainly helped tonight." She paused, then tilted her head, as if defying herself. "Mr. O'Grady, I don't remember seeing you around town before."

"I just arrived today, Miss Norgard. I'm testing the waters about buying a business here."

"Then I insist that you come to the house for dinner tomorrow night. It's the least we can do. About seven o'clock at our house on Minnesota Street. Where are you staying?"

He told her.

"Good. Now, if you men will excuse me, I want to get home and see if I can clean this new jacket or if I'll have to throw it away. Oh, dear, look at my skirt."

Canyon and Milt walked her to the Norgard home, two blocks south on Minnesota Street, which ran perpendicular to Main. From the house they could see a few night lanterns at the Norgard mill.

When Felicia was safely inside, Milt waved his hand. "I think it's time I thanked you again with a drink. Shall we find the nearest saloon?"

"Good idea. A beer would go good right now."

They stopped at a small saloon down a block on Minnesota near First and took a table. Nobody seemed to mind that O'Grady and Milt were both muddy. Some of it was starting to dry.

"Thought I heard a shot just before that horse panicked," O'Grady said. "Mr. Norgard, did you hear anything?"

"Yes, I heard it, too, and the name is Milt. Mr. Norgard is my father. The shot must have been close to the animal."

"Too close, or perhaps it hit the horse."

They tipped their cold beers.

"Since I'm new in town, could I ask you some questions?"

"Fire away."

"Mostly lumbering and sawmill work here, right?"

"Yes, the two big mills in town, and a dozen little ones scattered up and down the St. Croix River. Most of us float our logs in from well upstream."

"Any idea how your fire started last night?"

Milt looked up quickly, his face angry. "Damn good idea. Somebody from Rombold Lumber set it deliberately."

"Some bad blood between the two of you?"

"Goes way back. Fact is Rombold and my dad used to be partners here early on. Then Old Man Rombold swindled Dad out of his fair share, and Dad had to start over. Yeah, I guess you could say bad blood."

Norgard looked at O'Grady and lifted his beer. "Here's a heartfelt toast to you, O'Grady, for saving Felicia's life tonight."

They both lifted their bottles and drank.

"Still don't see how you got there so damn fast. I was sliding around in that mud like a scared shoat. For a second there I thought the horse had knocked both of you down."

"Sometimes the quickest way to get another yard or two is to dive. It worked this time. That front buggy wheel just grazed my boot."

"Maybe Dr. Potter should look at your shoulder," Milt said.

"No reason. If it's broken, I'll know it in the morning. Right now I need another beer."

O'Grady went to the bar, bought two more beers, and brought them back and gave one to Milt. He tipped the locally brewed beer, then looked at Milt. "Does the number ten have any special meaning here in Stillwater?"

"Ten, the number?"

"Right marked like a tally, four straight lines, the fifth crossed, and done again."

"Does sound like a tally, but it doesn't bring anything to mind. Why? Is it important?"

"Must not be. It's part of a puzzle a man made for me that I'm trying to figure out."

"Oh, I'm not much good on puzzles. What kind of business you said you're looking for?"

"Hardware. Always loved the hardware business."

"We've got a good store in town now, hardware and tinsmith combined. Good man running it."

"So I'll pick something else. I need to look around a bit."

Milt finished the second beer and stood. "I better be getting home. My wife doesn't like the music recitals, so I promised Felicia I'd take her. That's why we were out tonight. Now I better scoot. Why don't you drop by at the mill office tomorrow, so I can be sure you're not stove up somewhere."

"Be glad to. Yours is the mill to the south."

"Right, can't miss it."

They shook hands and Milt walked out. O'Grady watched a few hands of poker, then decided he could use some sleep.

Outside the saloon, he turned north to Main and swung to the left.

O'Grady saw where he had taken his dive into the muddy street and thought again about the pretty lady. Felicia reminded him of a tiny Dresden doll. One of those made of fine china. He was glad he would see her again.

Next to the Aces High Saloon was a vacant lot, and O'Grady took one precautionary look into the dark depths and quickened his pace a little as he went past the void. He was almost to the far side of the vacant area next to the general store when a shot blasted. He had no time even to flinch as he felt hot lead slamming past the side of his head.

He dived to the boardwalk, rolled on his good right shoulder, and came up behind the wall of the Maitland General Store. The gunman hadn't fired a second shot. Why not? There was time. O'Grady bent low and peered around the wall of the store at boardwalk level. He saw some movement in the darkness, but not enough to fire at.

Who in hell was shooting at him? O'Grady surged around the edge of the store low to the ground, knowing he was being silhouetted by the kerosene lights across the street. The next shot went high. He charged down the side of the building toward the muzzle flash, his new .38 revolver out of leather and looking for a target.

He didn't shoot at the flash because that would give away his position. For a few seconds he had the advantage. He stopped breathing and listened. He heard someone sucking in breath across the void against the saloon wall.

O'Grady closed his eyes, listening for movement. Nothing. When he opened his eyes and stared at the spot where the bushwhacker must be, he could see the outline of a light-colored shirt. O'Grady lifted the .38 caliber French-made *pistolet*, and fired.

As soon as he got off the round, O'Grady bolted ahead two long steps and stopped. He heard a wail of pain from the other man, then three rounds blasted from the man's .45 revolver. They all landed behind O'Grady's new position. He knelt against the general store wall.

"That was your fifth round, hard case. Give it up and walk out to the street, and you live."

Another shot thundered in the narrow space and O'Grady felt flesh burn on his side. then the gunman ran deeper into the darkness. O'Grady fired his last four shots at the departing figure.

No chance to catch him now. He could run either way in the alley behind the stores. O'Grady touched his side. Damp. Not soaking, but he'd been sliced open. Lucky it wasn't deeper. The slug must have gone in and out.

He took his neckerchief, folded it, pressed it against his side, and walked back to the street and down to his hotel. Once in his room on the second floor, O'Grady lit the kerosene lamp and checked his side.

It was deeper than he expected. He took the pillowcase off the pillow and tore it into strips, then he used part of it for a clean pad over the wound and tied it firmly in place around his torso. That would stop it bleeding and keep it safe till morning. Then he'd have to go get the wound cleaned and bandaged by Dr. Potter, after all.

The next morning after breakfast, O'Grady walked

to the doctor's office a block down on Minnesota Street toward the Norgard's big house. The doctor was in.

Potter looked at O'Grady's side and grunted. "Well, it's easier to treat than a sawed-off hand. Get some bad ones now and then from the saws and the axes in the woods. Who shot you?"

"Don't know, didn't see him. You treat a gunshot wound last night after eleven?"

"Fact is, I did. Young man got a bullet in his shoulder. Said he dropped his gun and it went off." Dr. Potter was in his late thirties and looked like a logger himself. He was tall and wide-shouldered, but his hands worked smoothly.

"You know the gent who got shot last night?" O'Grady asked.

"Fact is, I don't. Must be new in town, like you. I get to know everybody sooner or later."

"Could you describe him for me?"

"Why would I want to do that?"

"Because I was walking toward the general store last night and he bushwhacked me. The coward attacked me from ambush with no warning. Man like that deserves to be reported."

"Uh, huh."

"Was the slug you took out of him smaller than usual, about this size?" O'Grady took a round from his belt loop and showed it to the medic.

"Yeah, about that size. Damn, solid cartridges for a revolver? Don't see many of those."

"It's imported from France. What did the guy look like who tried to kill me?"

Dr. Potter stared at O'Grady a minute, then

shrugged. "I guess I should tell you. This gent seemed slick and sure of himself. He was maybe five-eight, slight, wore town clothes and shoes, not boots. Admitted that he wasn't much good with his six-gun but figured that he'd need one 'over here' for protection."

"That it? Anything more? What color is his hair, his eyes?"

"Black hair and brown eyes. No other scars I saw on his upper body. I bandaged his shoulder after taking out the slug. He put his shirt back on and a jacket. You won't see him showing a white bandage."

O'Grady thanked the doctor, gave him a gold piece for the bandaging, and walked out on the street. He hadn't been to the whorehouses yet. They were all on one street. The town fathers had dictated that early on. This was a family town. But the deputy sheriff said one of the whorehouses here used a red light in the window. It might fit the puzzle.

O'Grady took the walk. The houses of ill repute were lined up on the east side of Ohio Street, nearly a dozen. He walked up the block counting, then back down. He didn't see any red light in any of the windows. Maybe the girls weren't working today.

He checked his watch. It was too early. The women probably worked until four or five A.M. They had to get their beauty sleep sometime.

When he turned back on Main Street, his side hurt, and that made him think of the bushwhacker. Who in this town would want to kill him? He hadn't been here four hours when the shots were fired. The doctor said the bushwhacker must be new in town.

Nobody knew O'Grady was coming here, except maybe that one deputy sheriff in Minneapolis. No one else. Didn't make sense. Had someone seen him come out of Thorndike's house in Minneapolis and followed him here? Maybe someone saw him talking with the waitress and looking at the pictures.

If that were true, the man knew about the bonds and had probably killed Thorndike. O'Grady walked quickly to the end of Main out by the river and talked to the owner of the Stillwater Livery Stable.

"Yeah, I remember you. Came in last night from Minneapolis. You were the first, then somebody came in about an hour after you did. He didn't say where he was from."

"What did he look like? He might have been my buddy I was supposed to meet here."

"Let's see," the livery man said." He was not real tall like you, slight, kind of a dandy, wore a double-breasted vest, as I recall. Unusual. Town clothes and all. Yep, that was him. Paid me for a week's feed and stall."

"He give you a name?"

"Sure, said he was Rufus Thorndike."

5

Charity did a suggestive dance across her bedroom floor toward the bed, humping forward her large hips, shaking and waggling her bare breasts at Lon, and all the time making sucking sounds with her mouth.

"Luv, you know how all that gold money makes me just quiver and shake. I declare, I've never seen so much money since the time three of us girls stole the week's receipts from that bawdy house I worked at in Omaha and took off west. Denver was heaven. I don't know to this day how I wound up in a jerkwater town like Stillwater."

"Glad you did," Lon Cumberland said. He lay naked on her fancy pink bedspread smoking the longest, biggest cigar he could find in town. Had cost him twenty cents. He puffed and watched Charity shaking and humping. When she pushed forward with her hips that way, he could almost see her slot. Damn, she was a lot of woman. So she was a whore; to Lon, all women are whores one way or another.

"Get them tits over here, woman. I'm getting hungry again," Cumberland said. He opened his mouth.

The bed jolted as she sat down, then he shut his eyes and opened his mouth and waited.

"First tell me how many more bonds you printed today, you rich son of a bitch."

He snapped open his eyes, but she was just teasing. "I printed ten. With the two colors it's hard to get the register just right where one ink goes beside the next. They have to dry between printings. Yeah, lots of hard work."

"But at fifty dollars each, you made yourself—that is, you made us—five hundred dollars. That's more than all the girls I got make working all night."

"Yeah, but those whores love their work, you can't fool me." He grabbed one of her breasts and pulled her over to him.

"You said nobody had found out about the bonds yet, so nobody is hunting you, right?"

"Near as I can tell. That's why I went to Minneapolis to sell the first ten. If the federal guys come looking, it'll be in Minneapolis. That's why I want to find somebody in Chicago to sell the bonds. I can send them in the mail, a registered package. Yeah, and if they turn up all over the country, the damn U.S. agents will go crazy trying to find out where they come from."

He chewed on her big breast a minute. "You know half the fun of this whole latch-up is doing a quality printing job. Good as they can do in Washington with all their fancy equipment. The second great feeling is knowing that I'm putting a fast one over on the government. 'Course, I don't mind the money either."

"How much do you think we can make from the

bonds—say, before the government starts hunting you so hard you got to stop?"

"I dream of selling a thousand of them," Lon said.

"At fifty bucks each? Jesus!" She let out a soft whistle. "That's . . . that's fifty thousand dollars."

"Yeah, we can live in style with that much money. Move to New York, take the boat over to Paris and London."

"My, you got fancy ideas, Lon Cumberland, big fancy ideas. We could also use about ten thousand and buy a good bawdy house in Chicago and never run out of customers."

Cumberland scowled, then grinned. "Hell, yes. We might do that. If I keep you working, I can play the horses at the track and live it up."

"We could, sweet thing, *we* could. When *we* get that kind of cash I won't let you out of my sight." She watched him a minute. "You staying the night?"

"I'll be back. This afternoon there's some printing I have to do for a store in town. He's been yelling at me for a week to get it done. I got to do the jobs, otherwise somebody's bound to get curious."

O'Grady had been to the small print shop up the street from the one-man newspaper, but it was closed. So he went down the street to the sheriff's office. A sign on the door said, "This is a temporary building on the permanent location. Construction of the new stone Washington County Courthouse will get under way in June 1861."

The building sat in the center of a square city block bounded by Court Street and Minnesota and Michigan and A streets. That put it a block and a half from the center of the small town.

Inside, there was a sign that pointed to the county clerk's office and another arrow to the sheriff's office. When O'Grady opened the sheriff's door, a man looked up from a desk. There were two doors behind him, evidently leading into offices.

"Yes, sir?" the man asked.

"I'd like to talk to the sheriff," O'Grady said.

One of the two doors opened and Sheriff Rex Spurlock nearly filled the frame. He stared at Canyon's red hair and large frame.

"Mr. O'Grady, I presume. I was wondering when I'd meet you. You had quite a night last night from what I hear. First you save a lady from nigh onto certain death from a runaway horse and then you get bushwhacked over by Maitland's General Store. How's the side feeling?"

"Good to meet you, Sheriff. The side is just scratched. I need to have a short talk with you. Would right now be all right?"

"Now would be fine."

O'Grady settled into a chair in the office as the sheriff closed the door. The lawman took out a bottle from the bottom drawer and poured shots of whiskey into two glasses.

"I figure you being in town has something to do with a law-enforcement matter and that you must be a lawman, U.S. marshal, maybe. I've seen a few in my time and you have that manner about you."

O'Grady tossed down the shot of whiskey and savored the taste still in his mouth. It was good stuff. "That's good Irish whiskey, and you're partly right.

I'm a special federal agent working directly for President Buchanan.'' O'Grady presented a thin printed card that had a small tintype photo pasted to it. It identified him as a special agent for the president.

"That's a new one. Didn't even know there was such a job. You must be here on business." The sheriff watched him a moment, then tossed down his own shot of whiskey. "So?"

O'Grady briefed the problem for the sheriff quickly. "So far I don't know who I'm looking for or where. I don't know if this is a way station or if the bonds are printed here or if they come out of Chicago or Denver. I'm clutching at straws right now all because of a pictograph."

O'Grady spread out the drawings on the sheriff's desk. Two of them had smudges on them.

"That deputy in Minneapolis was right about the red light. We have one here at night. Ten, ten, what the hell is that?" The sheriff grinned. "I'll be damned. A small red lantern hangs in the window at the Charity House. That's on Ohio Street with the other brothels. And I just figured it out. Charity House is the tenth house from this end."

"Charity runs the place?"

"Indeed she does, all two hundred pounds of her on a five-foot frame. She must be forty years old by now. Still works when her girls get too busy. A real character, our Fat Charity is. But she couldn't be the brains to an operation like this. She's more greedy than smart."

"Who does she know?"

"Everyone in town. Half the men in Stillwater have been to see her from time to time."

"So that looks like a dead end. But why did Thorndike go to so much trouble if it wasn't important? Two references."

"I'm more interested in this bushwhacker. Your description was good and he's got a wounded left arm. Maybe we can track him down. You think he must have seen you in and out of this dead man's office?"

"That's the only connection we have so far."

"What are you going to do next?"

"Not sure. I'm about ready to lean back in one of those chairs outside the hardware store and take a snooze in the sun."

"Could be a permanent nap. We don't know where the killer is. Even if this bushwhacker isn't a good shot, he could walk right up to you."

O'Grady pulled one .38 round from his belt loop and tossed it to the lawman. "I've got one advantage. I can reload six or eight times faster than he can."

"Cartridges for a revolver?" the sheriff asked. "Damn, I've been wishing they would hurry on those. Where you get a weapon to fire them?"

O'Grady told him.

Ten minutes later, O'Grady was back on the street. It wasn't noon yet. His dinner date at the Norgard house wasn't until seven, and he could stop by at the Norgard lumber mill later. Now it was time to explore more.

He noticed a young man coming down the street. He looked a little strange and walked with a jerky, irregular motion. When O'Grady saw the man's round face, hooded, slanted eyes, and high forehead, he realized this was one of the slow people. Mentally he was sub-par. He'd known such a man once.

Two young boys ran out at the young man and screeched at him and jeered and laughed. The man stopped until they went away. He walked forward and the boys rushed at him again.

This time O'Grady was between them and the man. "What are you boys doing?" he demanded.

They stopped, eyes wide, looking at his gun. Few men on the streets of Stillwater wore guns.

"Nothing, mister," one boy said.

"We was just teasing," the other blurted.

"What you were doing is nasty and foolish. You boys run for home as fast as you can or I'm going to tell your mother what you did."

They looked at him, then down at his gun, turned, and fled.

When O'Grady turned around, the slow-witted man had stopped and watched him. He grinned at O'Grady, waved, and went on down the street with his arm-swinging walk that was half-stumble, half-fall.

O'Grady watched him and a short way down the street he turned in at a saloon. It was one of the smaller ones. O'Grady was curious. He went in the same saloon and asked for a beer at the bar. The young man was not in sight. Before O'Grady's beer was gone, the slow-witted man came out from the back room and began cleaning the spittoons and emptying them in a bucket.

O'Grady stood at the bar and motioned to the apron. "Who is the young swamper?"

"Him? That's Artie. He's a good kid, works for us here. We don't have any complaints. Does his job, he's never late, never sick."

Artie wiped out a spittoon and put it where it usually sat. Just then a man with one beer too many backed up, stepped in the spittoon, and fell over backward. He roared in anger and jumped up and charged Artie.

"I told you not to put that damn spitter there, you damn imbecile!" The drunk slapped Artie across the face and spun him around. "Damn you, Artie, you ruined my new shirt."

O'Grady moved swiftly and was just behind the man when he swung his hand back to hit Artie again.

"Got to teach you, Artie."

O'Grady caught the drunk's right hand from behind, jerked him around, and slammed a right fist into the man's stomach. Quickly a short left with all of O'Grady's weight behind it pounced into the man's jaw. The drunk started to double over from the belly shot, then was lifted off his feet when the left hit his jaw. He flopped over on his back on one of the sturdy tables and lay there, unconscious.

Two men in back clapped.

Artie looked at O'Grady and smiled. "Th-thanks," he said.

Canyon touched his low-crown brown hat in a salute and walked out the saloon door.

Maybe it was time he stopped down at the Norgard Sawmilling and Lumber Company. Milt might know more about the people in the town than he thought he did. A little judicious digging might turn up something.

O'Grady admitted he had discounted the idea that the perfect print job on the bonds could come from this one-horse, two-sawmill rough-and-tumble little town. It just didn't figure that a local printer would have that kind of equipment.

So maybe it was time he found out. He had been past Lon's Quality Printing before; maybe the printer would be there now. It was almost noon, and the shop was open. The business was in a building of its own, a small one, thirty feet wide and not much deeper than that.

As soon as O'Grady opened the street door, the smell of ink and paper hit him, and he grinned. It was a familiar perfume. He always wished he could be a printer. Presses fascinated him. The shop was small, had a partition across the back, where he guessed the printer might live or which he used for supplies. A short, thickset man looked up from one of the presses and waved. He printed another sheet, hand-feeding in the paper, then wiped his hands and moved toward O'Grady.

Everything was out in the open and up front. A small table to one side with a chair behind it served as the office, order room, and layout table. Two small platen presses stood between tables loaded with paper, print forms, and small boxes filled with customers' orders. A type case against the wall held two dozen fonts of hand-set type.

"Yes, sir. What can I do for you today?" the printer asked.

"I'm going to need some personal cards, business cards. I'm looking for a business here in town."

The man nodded. "About a hundred until you find your spot?"

"That should do it."

"What do you want on the card?"

"O'Grady Business Enterprises, Canyon O'Grady, Lumberman's Hotel. That should do it."

"I'm a little behind. I can have them done in four days. Will that be soon enough?"

"Have to be. Black ink is fine."

"What kind of type?"

"I'll let you put it together, you're the printer. I wouldn't know one kind of type from another."

"Good. I'll have them ready. White card stock?"

"Fine. Just so it looks good." O'Grady glanced around. "Print shops have always fascinated me. Don't know anything about the business, but looks like it would be satisfying."

The short chunky man with a fleshy face nodded. "True, printing can be a real art form, if a man has time to do it. Me, I'm too busy printing business cards."

O'Grady chuckled, looked around a little, and then waved and went back to the street. From what he had seen inside, that little print shop would be doing good to get out a well-printed sheet of business stationery.

Which left the last clue: the whorehouse. But that was night work. He consulted his big pocket watch. It was just after noon. He had a sandwich and coffee at a café and walked the street again, trying to put the puzzle together. The bushwhacker was here, that was for sure. He must have followed O'Grady. Did he know any more about this counterfeiting operation than O'Grady did?

An hour later he gave up on the street. He could check in at Norgard's sawmill; maybe the lumberman would have some ideas to help him.

O'Grady walked south on Minnesota Street, cut over to Michigan, and followed it to the sawmill property. A raw lumber building had a sign over the door that said OFFICE. O'Grady turned the knob and stepped inside.

It was a big room, with three desks. At the center one sat a woman bending over papers. She looked up.

A smile lighted Felicia Norgard's face, and she stood. "Oh, good, Mr. O'Grady, you did come. I want to thank you again for saving my life last night."

O'Grady smiled. She was as pretty as a butterfly on a buttercup. "Miss Norgard, that's kind of you. Looks like you didn't break any bones and that smudge of street mud even washed off your cheek."

"Oh, yes. I saved the clothes, too. They'll be fine. Milt said you might stop by. He should be back in a minute. Sit down here beside my desk and we can talk. I'm curious. How in the world did you ever get such an interesting name as Canyon?"

6

Roman Rombold sat at his desk in his private office at the Rombold Lumber Company on the east side of Stillwater. The mill and pond and yard stretched northward along the St. Croix River.

He was still furious over the loss of his resaw building, the saw itself, and a good quantity of finished lumber in the fire two nights ago. He knew that someone from the Norgard bunch had set the blaze in revenge for the Norgard fire, but there was no way to prove it. He personally had not ordered the fire in Norgard's stacks of drying lumber, but someone from his mill must have done it. He hadn't shed any tears when he heard about it, but it hadn't been a policy move by his company. Now he was faced with making some response to Norgard's action. His first reaction was to burn down the Norgard mansion on Minnesota Street, but the more he considered it, the less he favored it. It was too obvious.

That opened the feud up to family members, the women and children, and he didn't want it to go that far.

What the hell could he do?

Freeze them out would be ideal. But with all of

the stumpage available up the St. Croix, that would be virtually impossible. True, the ready-to-cut timber was getting to be farther and farther from the mills. But the St. Croix as a highway for log rafts worked just as well for forty miles as for four.

He threw a pencil across the room.

Pragmatically his best option was to burn down the Norgard mill, level it right to the ground. But then he would have to put up an eight-foot steel mesh fence around his own mill and hire 'round-the-clock shotgun guards stationed every fifty feet to avoid retaliation. That would double his cost of doing business.

Another option was to kill Milt Norgard. Milt was the source of the rougher tactics they faced from Norgard. He had the guts to get out and set a fire, or use a rifle and put a slug through a lookout's leg. Old Man Helmer Norgard would never do that. But the option of killing Milt didn't set well with Roman Rombold either. Murder was still a step too far.

Cornering the supply of logs still looked best. He would tell his advance timber buyer to go all out, bidding 5 percent over the going rate so he could tie up the close-in blocks of timber. That would be one good step. What the hell next?

Roman grinned as he thought of another move. His brothers might not like it, but they didn't have to know. He told the office manager he'd be gone for an hour or so, and checked in the dingier saloons along Main Street. He found his man at the fourth one and motioned him outside through the back door.

They walked down the alley. The first thing Roman did to gain the man's attention was to hand him three silver dollars. Lash Janson's bloodshot eyes widened, and he watched the mill owner with a new interest.

"I'm going to pay you to get into fights, Lash. As simple as that. I want you to mash up a few people so they can't go to work for a week or a month. Don't kill anybody, or I'll hire somebody to gun you down with a rifle. You understand?"

"Fight, yeah. Easy. Who?"

"Anybody who works for the Norgard mill or in their woods." Roman Rombold stared at the big man. Janson was six-six and weighed three hundred pounds, but he didn't even have a beer belly. He was thick all over, and fighting was what he did best. He'd been fired from every job he had in town for fighting on the job.

"I fight with guys who work for Norgard. How'll I know that?"

"Follow them from the mill. Shouldn't be hard. Follow them and yell at them and accuse them of hitting you or of spilling your beer in a saloon. Saloon fights are best. You must know a dozen men right now who work for Norgard's mill and woods."

Lash blinked and furrowed his forehead, then he nodded. "Yeah, but I like some of them."

"Tough, Lash, this is business. I'll pay you twenty dollars for every man you beat up so bad he's off work a week or more. Broken arms are the easiest. Remember, no killing."

"Hell, I start tonight."

"Don't be obvious about it," Roman said. "Pick the men you know who work at Norgard first. Be sure you don't get too drunk to do your job. You can drink up your profits later. Don't drink more than two beers a night. You understand?" He looked up into the huge man's blood-streaked eyes.

"Yeah, understand. Start tonight."

Roman Rombold patted him on the shoulder, turned away, and walked out to the street. When he looked back, Lash Janson was headed into the back door of a saloon.

The slight man with a bandage on his shoulder eased up from his bed in the Evergreen Hotel. His name was Druce Gorman and now he sat on the edge of the mattress and slowly raised his left arm with the elbow bent until it was shoulder-high. His face turned red with the effort and he bleated in pain.

"Damn shoulder," he muttered. He had work to do. That big redhead was in town ahead of him. They had exchanged shots and he got the worst wound of the pair. Gorman had looked out his window this morning and seen the damn redhead walking the streets.

The only good thing about it was that the investigator looked as puzzled as he had been the day before. Evidently whatever he took from the Thorndike house hadn't yet led him to the man who printed the plates for the bonds.

This sad little town must not be the right place. Druce had been inside Lon's Quality Printing shop, the only one in town. It didn't have a press that could print a good calling card.

Gorman lifted his shot-up left arm again and again, and gradually the pain ebbed to a mild ache and the arm felt a little better. If he went outside, he had to put his jacket on. That bandaged arm would be a huge bull's-eye for the redhead.

Gorman had checked out the newspaper printing plant as well. It had a hand-operated press that had to be fifty years old. So why did the big redhead come to Stillwater?

Something had to be here, maybe a clue of some kind. Those damn pictographs. They were all over the house that Thorndike used in Minneapolis. He had no idea they were the clues, not until the redhead took some out of the house and began talking to everyone about them.

Now what? If he killed the redhead, he might eliminate the one man who could lead him to the plates. Gorman pictured those engravings. The same size as real U.S. bonds, beautifully engraved, and all ready to go on a modern press and produce almost undetectable copies of U.S. treasury bonds. He began to sweat just thinking about it.

As a printer himself, Gorman knew what he could do with the bonds. He'd go to a major city, where he could get five or ten thousand of them sold within two days, then vanish with the cash and the plates and move to another big town.

He figured he could do the same trick three times before he had to toss the plate in the bottom of a river somewhere.

But first he had to find the damn engraved plate.

He looked out the window and saw the redhead walking down the street. A good rifle was all Gorman needed to end it right here, but he couldn't do that. He had planned on letting the redhead find the engraving, then killing him.

The shots last night had been a spur-of-the-moment thing. Now he wished he hadn't done it. The man would be doubly on the alert now.

Gorman went back to the bed and exercised his arm again. The more he worked it, the less stiffness would develop, the doctor had told him. As he lifted his arm up and down and around and around, he remembered when he had seen the first bond.

Thorndike had shown it to him that night when they played cards. He'd known Thorndike for five years and only lately had the confidence man got religion. Together they had had a good racket going, printing and selling diplomas from universities and colleges.

Most of them were from medical schools and a few were law degrees. Made good money. Out West a diploma on the wall was accepted at face value. It was a lot quicker to buy a diploma than to earn one.

Thorndike had showed him the bond and said this was going a little bit too far. Counterfeit treasury bonds could have serious consequences on the federal government. He mailed the bonds to the treasury department as soon as he found the second one with the identical serial number.

They had argued, and Thorndike wouldn't tell him a thing about where he got the bonds or who sold, distributed, and printed them. Shooting Thorndike had been a mistake. Now he didn't want to let his temper cause him to make another error.

He would keep close check on the redhead. With a hat pulled low, a bulkier jacket, and some thick spectacles, Gorman knew he could disguise himself enough that the redhead wouldn't know him if they met face to face.

First he would check at the other hotel, where the man stayed, and get his name for sure. Then he would find a place across the street to keep watch on the hotel. He had to know everything that the big redhead did. Yes, a start. As soon as the redhead found the engraver or the plates themselves, the big man was dead.

In the Norgard office, Canyon O'Grady took off his hat and sat in the chair Felicia motioned to.

"Enough of this 'Miss Norgard,' " she told him. "I'm Felicia and I want you to call me that. Now, how in the world did you get the Canyon name?"

"I picked it out myself just after the doctor gave me a spank on my bare bottom the day I was born," O'Grady said.

Felicia giggled. "You did not. Now tell me. I know your mother gave it to you, but why?"

"You're insisting? It's boring."

"Tell me."

"My parents both came to this country from Ireland. My father was one of the men who started the Young Ireland Movement and a good friend of Finlan Lalor and Padraic Pearse. In those days in Ireland, having two friends like those put you quickly on the British wanted-posters.

"My parents knew they had to come to America to get away from the British. Mother started reading all the books she could on America. She looked at all the pictures she could find as well.

"She was well along with me, then. She decided that Canyon should be my name. She said it symbolized for her the new, raw, wild land she was coming to.

"I was almost born in Ireland, but I waited until we got to dry land again in New York. So I became Canyon. Of course, the Irish parish priest would have nothing of the name, so on my christening paper I'm officially Michael Patrick O'Grady. But my parents and my friends never call me anything but Canyon."

"And now you're here to start a business, Milt tells me. What kind of a business?"

"Almost anything but women's shoes."

Felicia laughed this time. Her soft brown hair swung around as she let the laughter roll out. Dimples appeared and her hazel eyes glowed with joy. "Really, tell me, what kind of a business?"

"I've been thinking of starting a bookkeeping service for small firms. Think I could get enough customers?"

"I don't know . . ." She stopped. "You're teasing me again. Why don't you have an accent, an Irish brogue?"

"Sure 'en, lass, I can lay on a brogue so thick you'll have trouble understanding it." He lathered the sentence with as much Irish as he could get into it.

Felicia laughed again. "I think I like you better without all that accent. You're still coming to dinner tonight?"

"Of course. Wouldn't miss it."

"Good. I get to go home early to start cooking. Oh, here comes Milt. He says he's putting on three more night guards. I hope this war of fires doesn't keep going."

Milt waved and stopped in front of them. "O'Grady, good, glad you came. I have an idea. Come on in here where the lowly bookkeeping help can't hear us."

Felicia threw a wadded-up ball of paper at Milt, who caught it and tossed it back to her.

Inside the small office, Milt closed the door and sat behind his desk. He went right to the point. "O'Grady, from what you said, you're more or less free of any pressing duties. I'd like you to come to work for me for a few months. I've got a small problem. Stumpage."

O'Grady frowned. "What is stumpage?"

"Timber ready to be cut, timber rights. We buy large tracts of timber on a mountain or hill, and then cut it off and raft it down the river. Which means we have to plan ahead two or three years. I'm in a spot now where I need more stumpage, and I know that bastard Roman Rombold is going to try to tie up everything for sale he can find."

"Wrong man," O'Grady said. "I might not look like it, but I do have a timetable. I know nothing about lumbering. I might just as well buy you a forest of hickory sticks and cherry trees."

"Damn," Milt said. "Well, I tried. I know you'd make a great buyer, but if I can't talk you into it, we'll move on. How goes the retail-business prospects?"

"It doesn't. Milt, that's just a story to cover up what I'm really doing here in town. I'm an investigator working for a big outfit. Nobody else knows about it except Sheriff Spurlock, so keep it quiet. I figured you might be able to help me."

"At least that makes more sense. You don't look like a merchant type. What can I do?"

"What do you know about the printer Lon Cumberland?"

"Not much. He does what little printing we get done. He's good at it. Does fine with his old equipment. His father was a printer east a ways somewhere, and when the old man died, Lon put all the equipment on a wagon and rolled it west until he found a town without a printer."

"Anything else?"

"He's not a real sociable type. Doesn't get into church or clubs or merchant groups much. Kind of a loner."

"He married?"

"No. Bachelor, I guess."

"You're not much help, Milt. The newspaper. Does the publisher also do job printing?"

"No. He leaves that to Lon. Told me once that he had more work than he can do turning out four pages of newspaper a week. He does it all by himself, so that seems to figure."

"That closes a few doors, at least."

Milt rubbed his face with his hand. "Now you're getting me curious about what you're looking for."

"Puzzles do get interesting, but this is one that doesn't touch on you, which is why I could ask you the questions. Better you don't know my problem right now."

"Fair enough. You still coming for supper?"

"Wouldn't miss it. That sister of yours is a charmer."

"And extremely young."

"I know. She is perfectly safe around me, promise."

"Good. Wish she'd get married, but she says she's choosy."

"Best way." O'Grady stood. "I better get back to work. Seven o'clock at your house. I'll be there."

"Good hunting," Milt said, and waved.

O'Grady went back to Felicia's desk. She looked at him as soon as he left Milt's office. Her eyes sparkled.

"Oh, damn," Felicia said softly. "Right now is when I need something really bright and witty to say, and I can't think of a thing."

"Tonight you can let your supper cooking do your talking."

"Oh, I'll have thought of something by then." She smiled and the dimples popped in.

"I'm looking forward to tonight," O'Grady said. He waved his hat at the pretty girl and walked outside. He was restless; he felt bogged down, like he was getting nowhere. He had to stir them up, whoever "they" were.

He hadn't followed up on the whorehouse yet. O'Grady couldn't figure how a fancy crib house had anything to do with counterfeiting of government bonds. But right now he was willing to try anything.

The indirect approach first. He went back to the same saloon where he had met Patsy that first night in town. She was there hustling drinks. He gave her a quarter for a beer and pointed to the chair.

"The all-talk no-action man. Yeah, Red, I remember you."

"Patsy, you ever work for Charity?"

"Sure, half the girls in town have. That's basic training. I don't know much about her. She's a fat whore, stole her bankroll from a madam somewhere, and landed here."

"Sounds about right. She married?"

"Nah. I heard she was giving her ass away to somebody regular, but I can't remember who."

"Try, Patsy." O'Grady tapped a twenty-dollar gold double eagle on the tabletop.

"Don't distract me with money when I'm thinking. I don't do this very often. Goddamn, nothing yet. I'll ask around. Don't lose that double eagle." Patsy stood and bent over the table, letting her blouse swing open for free viewing. "You still looking for that free ride?"

"Never can tell, Patsy. Right now I better get over to Charity House and do some research. I'll check back later on to see how your memory is doing."

"Yeah, be careful over there. One of her girls has a knife she loves to use. Just don't get your prick chopped off."

"Not a chance."

Five minutes later he pushed open the white door of Charity House and stepped into the whore's plush, overdecorated parlor.

7

Canyon O'Grady had decided how he would handle it before he walked into the Charity House's "display" room. His plan might work, and if it didn't, it should at least stir up some action on the counterfeiter's part.

A chubby woman of no more than eighteen came through a draped door to the side. She wore only a robe, thin enough to give glimpses of breast and furred crotch, but leaving a little to be hoped for. She was grinning and sipping a glass of what looked like lemonade. Her face was rouged and lips red, but her eyes were dull and tired.

"Looking for something special, redhead?"

"I most certainly am, and nothing so young and immature as you. I want to see Charity. Please tell her that I'm here."

"No, no. You got it wrong, tall man. Charity ain't working today. She don't work much at all anymore. I'm better. Everybody says so." She humped her hips forward suggestively. "How about a ride?"

"I want to see Charity about business, not your so-called pleasure. Please tell her I'm here."

"It's all right, Flossy, I can handle it." The voice

came from behind another beaded curtain over a doorway, and the woman who came through fit the description he'd had. About forty, tired, too much makeup even for a whore, and fat beyond reason. She chuckled, her body shaking in the process.

"Damn, but you are a big one. What's this about business?"

"Is there somewhere private we could talk? I was given to understand that this is a most confidential matter."

Charity's eyes lit up for a minute and one eyebrow lifted. "Oh, maybe it's *that* business. Sure, right in here, my private office."

She held open the beaded strands and O'Grady stepped through into a small room with a desk, a chair, and a couch. She was ready for any kind of business.

He waited until she sat down, then leaned toward her. "I was told to talk to you and tell you that things are selling beautifully and we need another fifty."

Charity grinned. "Oh, my, yes, now that *is* business."

"Then you understand what that means. I don't. I was hired simply as a personal messenger and told to come here and talk to you and give you this message."

"Absolutely. I know what it means, and you came to the right place."

"Fine, that's good to know. Let's see, there was more. I was told to say that prospects look good for branch offices in Chicago, Omaha, and Kansas City. I don't have the slightest idea what that means, but I assume that you do."

"Now you really do bring good news. Your message is understood. When will someone pick up the merchandise?"

O'Grady frowned and squinted his eyes, then he rubbed his chin and at last remembered. "Oh, yes, he said as soon as possible. He asked if you would write out the delivery date and seal it in an envelope, which I'll take back as proof that I delivered the message, and to communicate with him the delivery date." O'Grady wiped his brow. "Golly, I remembered all of it."

Charity frowned slightly. "Now that delivery date is going to take some time, an hour or so at least. Why don't you have a free poke while you're waiting? Flossy would like to get your pants off. No charge, and when you're fucked out, I'll have the envelope ready."

"Oh, my goodness, no. I'm sorry, but I'm a married man and I am faithful to my wife. I couldn't possibly fornicate. However, I do need something to eat. I'll go to a café and be back here in an hour."

Charity nodded, her face showing worry. "Well, if you got to. But you better make it two hours. Not sure I can make connections that fast. What time is it?" She looked at a clock on her desk. "Two-fifteen. You be back here at four-fifteen." She stood.

"Yes, ma'am, I'll do that." He looked at her once more, then fled out the beaded curtain, across the parlor, which now held three scantily clad women, and through the front door. He walked quickly until he was out of sight. Then he cut through the alley between two other adjacent whorehouses and walked cautiously along toward Charity House's back door.

There probably was no man in Charity House. She would have to use one of her girls as a messenger. He figured she had to contact someone else, someone not in the house. That was why it would take so long. That was why he was in the alley.

He found some bushes and brush and stepped into it. There was no house built behind the eighth whorehouse. He settled down so he could see the alley and the back door at the tenth house, and waited.

Most whores in houses kept off the streets as much as possible. The proper women of the town tended to insult them and chastise them, so the soiled doves usually walked up and down the alleys and used back doors when they needed to go out. O'Grady hoped that held true here.

He waited ten minutes and nothing happened. He figured Charity would have to write a note to someone. Evidently he had struck gold with his stumbling-bumbling-messenger routine. If sales were in Minneapolis, they would need some form of communication. A sly counterfeiter would certainly not put anything in writing that could be used as evidence against him.

The messenger seemed the best way. O'Grady knew he was taking a chance going into Charity House. The woman might have denied any knowledge of any merchandise other than her own girls. She could have thrown him out without a word and stopped his investigation.

Now at least he knew that Charity House was part of the scheme. He hoped that would lead him to the engraver, the plates, and any more printed bonds.

Fifteen minutes after he started waiting, he saw the rear door of Charity House open and a woman come out. She was small and young. She was properly covered in a long dress and a dark-blue jacket as well as a big hat that shaded most of her face. Her high button shoes were freshly shined. In one hand she clutched a white envelope.

O'Grady grinned and let her get half a block ahead before he stepped from the brush and followed her. She continued through the alley to the end of the block, went across A Street and into the alley again. She looked behind her once, but O'Grady had time to step in back of a buggy.

Then she seemed to hurry a little faster. When she came to the Lumberman's Hotel side door on the alley, she darted inside. O'Grady ran then, slammed through the door of the hotel, knowing he was too late. She could have gone into any one of thirty rooms, or scooted out the front door and gone either direction down Main. Dammit!

He checked out the hotel's front door looking for the small woman with black hat and blue jacket, but he couldn't spot her either way along Main. He leaned against the overhang post of the hotel and waited. Maybe she was hiding somewhere, waiting until he left or went the wrong direction.

A half-hour later he had seen nothing of the small woman. She had completely outfoxed him. By now her letter must be delivered.

That brightened O'Grady's day. If Charity had sent a note ordering fifty more bonds, then the man who printed them, and the engraved plates, both must be right here in Stillwater.

Progress of a sort, but not the best kind. He should have grabbed the girl and made her tell him where she was going. He also could have read the note. There could be some kind of salutation or name that would be helpful. Too damn late for that now.

O'Grady jogged up the alley to A Street and positioned himself halfway between the alley and Ohio Street, where the whorehouses fronted. The girl would have to go back to Charity House. Then she would tell Charity that someone had followed her. She would describe O'Grady, so there was no use going back at four-fifteen to get the delivery date. His mistake in letting the girl get away would also alert the counterfeiters that he was interested in them. They wouldn't know if he was a lawman or someone trying to steal the plates.

O'Grady waited until six o'clock and the girl hadn't returned. At least she hadn't come back from this end of the street. Knowing he would be watching for her, she probably simply walked north to Court Street and came to Charity House from the other end of the alley.

Damn, he had it right in his grasp and let it get away. There had to be another way. Just what it was, he didn't know. One fact came out clear: if they printed the bonds here in Stillwater, he needed to take a closer look at the two places in town that did printing. That would be night work.

O'Grady went back to his hotel room and tried to sort out the rest of it. His stab in the dark at the double clue of the whorehouse in the pictograph had turned into gold. He knew the bonds were printed here in town, or at least this is where they were ordered. A big step forward.

After midnight he'd check on the newspaper. It had the one big newspaper press, but there could have been a smaller one in back. And maybe the newspaper press would work for a finely engraved plate. He'd find out . . . tonight.

At six-thirty, he shaved closely, splashed on some witch hazel and bay-rum shaving lotion, put on a black jacket and string tie over his white shirt, and went out for dinner.

He arrived at the Norgard house five minutes until seven, and found Felicia waiting for him at the door.

"I was afraid you weren't coming," she said, and touched his arm. Her eyes were bright with excitement.

"I try never to disappoint a beautiful lady," he said.

"Oh, now," she said, then took his arm and walked with him into the parlor. It was understated, elegant, tasteful, and at the same time looked comfortable.

"Now, you sit right here and read the latest edition of the Chicago newspaper. We get one every afternoon when the freight line brings over goods from Minneapolis." She stood there a moment watching him.

"I'll read it," he said.

She giggled. "No, it wasn't that. I just wanted to look at you for a minute." Then she turned away. "Oh, dear! Usually I'm not so forward, especially with handsome men." She smiled at him over her shoulder and hurried into the kitchen.

He watched her trim figure and the delightful swing of her hips as she walked away. Now, that was going to put a man's word to the test. He had told Milt that Felicia was perfectly safe with him.

The front door opened and someone came in. A moment later two men walked into the parlor. Milt lead the way, saw O'Grady, and grinned.

"You made it. Good." He turned toward the sturdy man in his fifties who followed Milt.

"Canyon O'Grady, like to have you meet my father, Helmer Norgard, the man who put the company together, twice."

Helmer held out his hand and O'Grady saw that it had calluses and scrapes and cuts. He was a working man's boss.

"Good to meet you, O'Grady. Felicia hasn't talked about anything else since you swept her out of the way of that runaway buggy. My thanks for that brave move."

"I just happened to be there."

They sat down and talked.

"I tried to hire O'Grady to buy stumpage, Dad. But he's got another job right now."

"We need a good man up there. If we don't find one in a week or so, I'm going to have to go up myself."

"Not a chance, Dad. I'll go up. You've surveyed enough timber in your life. My turn."

Felicia came into the parlor flushed from the kitchen heat.

"We're ready to eat," she said.

It was a meal O'Grady would remember: steak and fresh oysters with six side dishes of vegetables, a huge pot of mashed potatoes, steak gravy, and lemon meringue pie.

"Now that's a supper that goes into my record book," O'Grady said as they finished. "Never before have I had steak and oysters together. A nice combination. I'm going to sneak off with the rest of that lemon pie."

Felicia grinned and beamed and shooed them out of the kitchen. "No doing dishes. I can do them anytime. Let's go out on the porch and talk."

It was pleasant on the screened porch, which overlooked the river. Felicia brought out second cups of coffee. Helmer left after a few minutes and then Milt said he had to look over some projections on their cutting schedule.

O'Grady mentioned that he should be going, too.

Felicia stood and moved close to him. "Before you go, do me a favor. Complete my education. I've never been kissed by a real redhead before." She stretched up toward him and O'Grady decided in an instant that one kiss wouldn't endanger her.

He put his arms around her and kissed her firmly and felt her against him, her breasts taut against his chest. It lasted longer than he had intended, and when their lips parted, Felicia sighed softly and blinked her eyes open and looked at him.

"Thank you," he whispered, then let her go and stepped back.

"When will I see you again?" she asked.

"I'll be here a week, maybe more. Maybe we can have dinner some noon at a café?"

"I'd like that, Canyon. How about tomorrow noon?"

He laughed, agreed, and departed.

As he walked back toward his hotel, O'Grady had a strange feeling someone was following him, but he couldn't find anyone in the darkness behind. He even stepped into an alley and waited five minutes, but no one came past looking for him.

He went in the side door of the Lumberman's Hotel and up to his room. He waited in the hall for another two or three minutes, but no one seemed interested in his movements.

His key unlocked the door and he stepped out of the faint lamp-lit hallway into the blackness of his room.

O'Grady struck a match and reached for the lamp on the dresser.

That was when he heard the sigh.

He swung the match around to light the bed and saw a woman lying there, half-undressed.

"Good. You finally got here. I been waiting all evening."

O'Grady had started to draw his six-gun, then stopped. He recognized the voice. He lit the lamp, turned down the wick, and put the chimney on.

With the improved light he saw Patsy lying there on the bed watching him. She wore a chemise and short silk bloomers that clung to her tightly.

"You're early, Patsy. It isn't pleasure time yet."

"I'm ready."

"I'm not. I do lots of my work at night." O'Grady watched her slowly slink out of the chemise, her breasts swinging gently, two perfect bells waiting to be rung.

"Make you a deal, Patsy. You hold on to your bloomers for an hour or so, and I'll be back and we'll have an all-night party. How does that sound?"

"I can wait. The question is, can you?" She lifted up on her knees on the bed and slowly pulled down her soft silk bloomers until they fell around her knees.

O'Grady chuckled. "You know all the ways to trap a man, little lady. But I've got a previous engagement. I'll be back here in an hour."

8

Canyon O'Grady moved through the night like an earthbound black bat, easing from cover to cover smoothly, making no sudden movements to attract attention. He left the hotel by the alley door and went forward to Main Street, then paced casually east past Minnesota Street and down to Michigan. There were no lights on in the small newspaper office when he passed it.

He turned down Michigan and came to the newspaper plant at the rear door. He checked the lock. A simple one, but as he pressed on the door, he could feel it bend in and touch a solid bar. No chance there. To the west side of the building lay a vacant lot. Two windows showed on that side, one near the back.

The sash window had been lifted two inches for some ventilation in the rear of the building, and no one had closed it when locking up. O'Grady placed a wooden box under the window, tugged it upward, and went inside the newspaper back room headfirst. He let his eyes adjust to the near darkness and found he was just above a bench filled with back issues of the paper.

He eased down on them, rolled off the bench, landing on his feet, and stood stone-still listening. Nothing moved. He made a quick inspection to be sure he was alone, then found a lamp, lit it, and turned it down low. He carried it from place to place.

The press interested him the most. It was a flat bed press designed to print one standard newspaper sheet at a time. It had to be hand-fed and power for printing was a long, wooden, well-worn lever. The harder the lever was pushed down, the better the print impression.

This was not the kind of press needed to print the treasury bonds. Wouldn't do the job.

Now he looked in corners and under tarps and stacks of paper. How could one editor/publisher be so messy? It looked as if he never threw anything away.

O'Grady worked the search systematically, moving in a straight line from one side of the room to the other. Type cases, five-gallon cans of ink, boxes of newspaper-size cut newsprint, pied type waiting to be sorted and returned to the type case, big wooden letters for headlines.

After an hour of moving systematically through the jumble, O'Grady blew out the lamp and replaced it. Nothing. Not a damn shred of evidence that the bonds had been, or even could be, printed there. One suspect down, one to go.

He went out the same window he entered and pushed it back down to the same two-inch opening, moved the box, and then walked out to Main Street. Nothing. He wanted to stop at a saloon and play some cards to forget the whole thing for a while. Maybe that would spark his brain cells.

Then he remembered Patsy. She would be good. Whores were the best when they weren't working, just making love. He thought of Patsy, then he thought of Felicia. Maybe a good long session with Patsy would help him keep his hands off the tempting Felicia.

He went into the hotel through the alley door and up to his room on two. When he opened the door, the lamp was still on. Patsy lay on the bed, undressed and smoking a cigarette.

O'Grady laughed. "That's absolutely the worst-looking rolled cigarette I've ever seen. Who taught you how to do that?"

"One of my admirers. He always liked a smoke afterward. That was a year ago. Now I like a smoke before, during, and afterward. Are you shocked?"

"Nothing any woman ever does can shock me."

Patsy sat up suddenly, which sent her breasts into a bouncing, jiggling tattoo. "Now, that sounds like a challenge." At once she changed her mind. "What the hell, I'm not here to entertain you. It's your turn to do good to me. Hell, it's free. What more can you ask?"

O'Grady sat down on the bed beside her. She was what some men call "comfortable," a woman with a little meat on her bones so her sharp places didn't poke into a man. Her breasts were medium-sized, but so perfectly rounded that they seemed larger. Her areolae were smaller than some and light brown, as were her nipples. He reached over and caressed one nipple and she moaned. "Oh, yes. Touch me there."

With one hand caressing Patsy's breast, Canyon lowered his lips to the other nipple and drew the firm tip into his mouth. Delicately, teasingly, his tongue danced around the light-brown circle of firm flesh. Patsy's moaning grew louder and she used both hands to clasp Canyon's head to her bosom. "Oh, yes, yes," she sighed, "that's it."

He moved his mouth to the other breast, licking the lush mound with his tongue while his fingers teased her still-wet other nipple. Now Patsy's hands were roving across Canyon's back, feeling his tightly muscled torso. Her nails dragged across the fabric of his shirt, setting his nerves aflame. He felt a red-hot flush of passion rise up from his groin and suddenly he was hard.

Patsy was panting now, her breasts heaving in excitement. "You set me on fire, redhead," she moaned. "I want you."

He drew back from her and quickly pulled off his clothes. Patsy leapt off the bed and faced him. Placing her hands on his shoulders, she pushed Canyon back onto the bed and lay atop him. Her stomach covered his crotch and her face landed in the middle of his chest. Grinning, she began to grind her belly into his crotch, up and down, side to side. Her eyes locked onto his and she smiled as she saw the pleasure she was giving him. Then, with a devilish look she licked her lips and placed her mouth over Canyon's right nipple.

Patsy sucked at the tight, firm flesh of his chest. Canyon was amazed as the waves of pleasure from his crotch seemed to increase, as if Patsy had packed more gunpowder into her bullets. At first she just sucked and licked, but then her teeth began to tease his nipple, and with each little bite he bucked his hips upward, rubbing himself against the satiny skin of her stomach.

She had wrapped her legs around one of his, and as she gyrated, he could feel her moist mound brush against him. It even seemed that he could feel the hardened button of her knob of pleasure dancing up and down his thigh. "Dammit, woman," he gasped. "You're amazing."

Patsy laughed from deep in her throat and then slowly began licking her way from his chest down along the sleekly muscled flesh of his belly. As her tongue darted in and out of his belly button, her hands found his solid, throbbing maleness. She cupped his sack in one hand while the other grasped the base and squeezed. He spasmed and for a moment thought that the time had already come, but then her mouth was down over the shaft.

Her tongue twirled along the underside until he hit the back of her mouth. She shifted the position of her head and suddenly she had him fully in her throat. It felt as if she was vibrating, and then he realized that she was swallowing over and over, tightening the muscles of her throat in wave after wave that sent surges of pleasure through his groin.

Patsy moved her hand from his sack to the hardened bridge of flesh below. As she continued to swallow, her thumb rocked back and forth across the rise. With each completed pass he felt his buttocks clench and once again he feared he was about to lose himself.

"Enough," he gasped. He grabbed Patsy under her arms and pulled her up. For a moment she looked concerned, worried that she had displeased him. But as he guided her into position above him, she saw the lust burning in his eyes. Slowly she settled back, taking the wet length of him in a gyrating motion, so that even this most primal of experiences seemed different.

"Yes, oh yes," she moaned. "This is what I wanted. Oh, yes . . ." She continued the circular motion, leaning forward to bring her clitoris more directly in contact with his shaft. Now she began rising and falling, pulling her hips back slowly, then rushing forward. Canyon put his hand behind her head and pulled her mouth down to his. His tongue pushed inside and he could feel her heaving breaths as her pace increased.

Patsy tried to moan, but Canyon's tongue invaded her mouth as deeply as he had invaded her below. When he felt the fast, hard tightening of her walls and he knew that her moment had come, he kept her lips pressed tightly to his, so that her gasps and moans came into his mouth, for him alone.

She pulled away for a moment when the gasping subsided, but her gyrations increased. Now Canyon was bucking his hips, rising up to fill her. She saw the glassy look come into his eyes, and as the first surges of him filled her, she pressed her lips against his once more and took from him the same impassioned breaths that he had claimed from her. He was aware of her everywhere—around his cock, her breast rolling against his chest, her lips and tongue mingling with his—until there was nothing else.

When O'Grady woke up in the morning, he was smiling. It had been an interesting night. Patsy was gone. He had figured she would be. She probably had some thinking to do. She had a hard life.

He went for breakfast as soon as the Northern Café down on Main Street opened for business. He was trying to put together his schedule for the day. Lon Cumberland's print shop was high on the list. Maybe he should watch the Charity House rear door. Chances were that Charity's boyfriend would be going in there, not the other way around.

It was a thought. He had just left the café after a big breakfast when he heard a bell ringing.

"Fire," a man bellowed as he ran past. A dozen more on the street hurried south in the direction of the Norgard sawmill. O'Grady ran with them. He just hoped it wouldn't be another round of arson fires. Sawmills were fire-prone enough without any help.

By the time O'Grady got to the mill three long blocks away, there were twenty men running with him. Nowhere could they see any fire or smoke.

A man stumbled out of the sawmill proper. He had blood across his face and down his chest. He screamed and staggered, then fell.

"Get Dr. Potter," O'Grady bellowed. He saw a younger man and pointed at him. "You, go find Doc Potter and get him down here right now."

Two more men staggered out of the mill, blood smeared all over.

O'Grady ran for the mill entrance. He hadn't heard an explosion. What the hell had happened here to create such a bloodbath?

9

O'Grady raced into the main part of the mill where the logs were cut by a large circular saw driven by a waterwheel.

The main saw and the carriage that pushed the logs through the spinning saw were both silent. A man lay against the carriage unable to move. One of his legs had been sliced off. Two more men sat nearby holding their arms, which looked like they had been shredded by shrapnel from an exploding artillery shell.

O'Grady looked for the main saw. Where was it? He ran to the spot and saw only a fragment of it left. Still dogged down on the carriage was a two-foot-thick pine log partly sawed. Glistening steel spikes driven deep into the log through the bark showed plainly where they had been chewed on by the spinning saw blade.

One of the men holding a bleeding arm looked at O'Grady. "Saw hit the big spikes and exploded like a cannon round. Sharp, jagged steel flew all over and to hell around here. Christ, I'm lucky to be alive."

O'Grady pulled off his shirt, cut it into strips, and

gently bound it around and around the man's bleeding arm. At last he got the bleeding stopped. He looked at the next man, who slumped nearby. Both his arms were bleeding, but they were minor injuries.

"Hold these folds of cloth over the bleeding, it should stop," O'Grady told the man. He looked at the third victim, with one leg missing. He was unconscious.

"My God," Dr. Potter rasped as he ran up and knelt beside the one-legged man. "You," he said, pointing to O'Grady, "help me with a tourniquet."

The doctor put on a tourniquet and found a foot-long stick to put through it to twist.

"Turn that tight as you can. We don't have to worry about anything but stopping the blood." He sent a millhand to find some metal and get it as hot as he could in the burner, and bring it back. "We got to cauterize that stump, or he's a goner," Dr. Potter said.

The man was still out. The doctor went to the two men O'Grady had patched, nodded at them, and said he'd be back.

"Anybody else hurt?" Dr. Potter called. "Anybody see a man who needs help?" he bellowed.

A call came from the other side of the main saw. The doctor ran that way.

O'Grady tightened the strap around the man's thigh again. The bleeding had almost stopped. A pool of red wetness soaked into the sawdust and splinters on the floor. He looked at the wounded man. A little color was creeping back into his face.

The one-legged man's eyes fluttered, then came

open, and the man screamed. It caught O'Grady by surprise and he dropped the tourniquet handle.

The scream trailed off as the man passed out again from the shock and pain.

O'Grady got the tourniquet back in place as Dr. Potter ran up with a six-inch-wide slab of iron that had lost its redness but still smoked. The doctor held it with a pair of metal tongs. He looked at O'Grady, then pushed the hot metal against the stub of the man's thigh.

The flesh sizzled, curls of smoke rose. The medic did it three times to cover all of the raw flesh, then he checked the stump and nodded. "He's getting some color back. Good job with the strap, keep it tight for a while more."

Then Dr. Potter was gone to wrap up another of the injured.

A half-hour later six men had been taken by wagon to the doctor's office. One man died of massive head injuries.

O'Grady, bare-chested now, stood near the main saw rig with Milt Norgard and his father. Both were shocked, disbelieving, angry.

Helmer Norgard shook his head. "The Rombold brothers would not do something like this. I'm sure of it. Milton, I don't want any action taken against their mill. Nothing. I'll have a talk with them this afternoon. They would never drive spikes and steel bars into logs. They know how dangerous it can be."

"But, Dad—"

Helmer held up his hand. "Let me talk with the

boys. I'd like you to come along. I'm sure they didn't do it."

"Then who did, Dad?"

"Have you had to fire anybody in the last two or three months?" O'Grady asked.

Helmer looked at his son.

Milt nodded. "Sure, there's always one or two. As I remember, we had to let three men go. One of them kept reporting late for work. He was late every morning for two weeks. On his job it slowed down our whole operation. One other guy I had to fire because he was a drunk. He drank twenty-four hours a day, even had a bottle on the job with him. The third one was just a kid and more interested in hunting and fishing than working."

"Get the names for me," Helmer said. "I'm going to see if I can find them today. I want some answers." Helmer turned and headed for the office.

Milt went back to the main saw and supervised the two men who were unbolting the shattered remains of the blade and getting ready to put on a new one.

"She just got filed last night, Milt," one of the men said as they lifted the new saw into position.

Milt approved and stepped back to where O'Grady watched the work. "Dad is wrong, mind my word. Roman is a rotten bastard. I'm sure he put somebody up to this. The stakes went in last night. That log was the second one on the chain to be sawed this morning. Somehow they got in here, went around the guard, and drove those bolts into place."

"Show me where the log was last night," O'Grady said.

They walked over to the head of the mill, where the logs came up a long V-shaped trough with a lugged chain in the bottom.

O'Grady checked the wooden trough and the ground near it. "If the rods were driven into the log last night, why didn't the guards hear the hammering? Steel on steel is loud."

Milt shrugged.

O'Grady pointed to three piles of sawdust and curls of wood under the next log on the chain. "There's the answer. Looks like they used a hand drill and a long bit; they drilled holes, then pounded the rods and spikes into the holes with a mallet or a length of wood. Makes almost no sound."

Milt slammed his fist into his open palm. "Goddamn! I'm going to get Roman Rombold if it kills me."

The rest of the mill crew were busy putting the main saw shed back into operating condition. They had to brace up two roof supports that were damaged by the flying, shattered saw blade.

Helmer came out and told the men they'd start sawing again tomorrow at noon. At ten the next morning they were all expected to be at the cemetery for the funeral service for Ralph Adler. He was the head rigger who got the log set and dogged down for the main saw. He'd just finished and was moving beside the carriage as the big saw hit the spikes and shattered. He didn't have a chance.

All but the repair group were sent home for the rest of the day.

O'Grady walked with some of the men as they headed back to town. They knew Adler. He was described as a good man.

O'Grady went directly to his hotel and pulled a new shirt from his bag and put it on. He added a Western vest and set his low-crowned, wide-brimmed hat in place.

It was after eleven when he looked at his watch and remembered his date with Felicia. He walked back to the mill and went up to the office.

Felicia had been crying. She wiped her tears, put on a light jacket and a soft hat, and reached for his arm.

Neither of them said a word until they were halfway to town.

"I'm sorry about the saw and the injured men," O'Grady said.

Felicia gasped a couple of times so she wouldn't cry, and looked at him.

"Why does it always have to come down to fighting? I saw Milt, and he's so angry he's about ready to explode himself. Before he came in, I found the revolver in his drawer and the two rifles and hid them. Milt has a temper. Sometimes he has trouble controlling it."

"Maybe this will be the time he does."

"I don't know. One of our men was beat up in a saloon fight last night, couldn't come to work. Milt talked to him and he said this big lummox, Lash Janson, picked a fight with him, pushed it and pushed it. Milt thinks Roman might have paid the guy to beat up our man."

"That could happen. But that's a long way from spikes in a log that's going into the main saw. The person who did that knew it could get somebody killed. He did it anyway."

"Milt talked to the big bully. He worked for us for a while. Milt held his six-gun on the man and told him if anybody from the Norgard mill or woods gets beat up from now on, Milt is coming after Lash. My brother said he had the giant shaking in his hobnailed boots."

"Let's hope that's the last of that."

They went into the Northern Café and had soup and a sandwich.

Gradually Felicia relaxed and finally smiled. "At least the lunch and the company is fine," she said. "How is your project going? Milt said you had something you were working on, but he didn't say what."

"It's progressing. I better get you back to the office. I don't want Milt coming after me."

They grinned and started back.

Halfway down Main Street they saw a crowd. As they came closer, they could hear loud voices.

"One sounds like Milton," Felicia said. She ran forward and elbowed her way through the four-deep circle of mostly men. In the center stood two men glaring at each other.

One was Milt, the other Roman Rombold.

"I don't care what the hell you say, Norgard. I didn't have anything to do with those spikes."

"Hell you didn't. If you were a man, you'd admit

it and pick up that ax and have it out right here," Milt threw the challenge.

O'Grady saw the faller's double-bitted ax lying on the ground near Roman. Milt had one like it in his hands. They stood six feet apart, bellowing at each other.

"Then why don't you admit you almost burned down our sawmill a couple of nights ago? Completely ruined the resaw building and the saw and about five thousand dollars' worth of lumber."

"Won't admit nothing to a killer like you, Rombold. You killed one of our men today, cost another man his leg, and we don't know who else might die. You're a killer!"

"Drop the ax and say that again, you bastard," Roman screamed.

"Let's do it with the axes, that way I have one less Rombold bastard to fight 'cause you'll be chopped into kindling within five minutes."

O'Grady saw the sheriff turn the corner and head toward the gathering. He wasn't rushing any.

"You want to try it man-to-man, drop the ax. I'm coming at you unarmed. You hit me with that ax, I'll have you in prison for ten years."

Rombold charged.

Milt dropped the ax and punched Rombold in the face twice. Milt danced away and Rombold rushed in again. Milt kicked Rombold's legs out from under him and Rombold rolled in the dirt.

"Come on, killer. You wanted fists, you got fists," Milt crowed. "Get up and fight!"

He did. Roman was more careful this time; he threw a punch and then drove straight ahead, catching Milt around the waist and slamming him into the dried-out street. Milt bucked him off and both leapt up.

From there on it was all Milt's advantage. He boxed like a bare-knuckled prizefighter, stabbing and jabbing with a wicked left hand, then pounding a hard right fist into Roman. The older man was not in good condition, spending all of his time in the office. Milt was all over the mill and the woods, and with the advantage of being four years younger, he wore down his rival.

The sheriff had seen the axes, but when it turned into a fistfight, he sauntered the other way.

Milt bore in again, slashed a left jab at Roman's nose bringing a gush of blood. He followed that with a powerful right fist that slammed into Roman's jaw. By that time, Milt's left hand powered into the side of Roman's face. His eyes glazed, his knees buckled, and he slowly sank to the ground, then sprawled on his face in the dirt, unconscious.

Two men from the Rombold mill picked up Roman and carried him off in the direction of Dr. Potter's office. The crowd, which had been mostly silent, began to break up now that the entertainment was over.

"Better than the fistfights we see in a ring," one of the watchers said.

Milt stood there weaving a bit, watching the people leave. Felicia and O'Grady hurried up to him.

"Glad you didn't use the ax," O'Grady said.

Milt turned slowly and looked at them. One of his knees buckled, but he kept standing.

"Daddy's going to be plenty mad," Felicia said. "He told you he wanted to talk with them."

"We talked," Milt said, holding up his fists, which had skinned knuckles and splotches of Rombold blood. "We talked with our fists. Now we'll see what tune Roman plays."

O'Grady grabbed Milt before both knees buckled, put his arm around the man's back and under Norgard's arm, and angled him down the street toward the mill.

Helmer Norgard watched the trio come in the office door.

"I heard about it," Helmer said. "So you won. What does it prove? How does it help? I found some interesting information about our friend Latimer Kincaid. He's the drunk we let go about six months ago. He hasn't had a job since. He's been heard in one saloon after another blaming us for his sad state. Says we're blacklisting him with other mills. The man has built up a big hate. I think he's the one who torched our lumber and who put those steel rods and spikes into that log last night."

Milt sat down in a chair and slumped over on the desk. "God, I hope it's him. I don't want to have to fight Roman again."

"What happens next?" O'Grady asked Helmer.

"I made a complaint to the sheriff. He's picked Kincaid up at one of the saloons and is questioning him about where he was last night. Then he'll check Kincaid's place for steel bars and big spikes and a long hand drill. Chances are we'll find enough to convict him. Sheriff said it will be manslaughter-

and-assault, and if somebody else dies, it could be a murder charge."

"Oh, damn," Milt said from where his face lay against the desk. "Wish I'd known about that an hour ago."

Helmer shook his head. "I told you I was on it. Told you I wanted to talk with the Rombolds first. You might be over thirty, Milt, but you still have a hell of a lot to learn about how to run a woods and a mill."

Milt pushed himself up so he sat in the chair. He looked at his father, his face showing two big bruises and one eye starting to close.

Helmer snorted. "Suggest you go down to the millpond and dunk your head a couple of times. Then I want you to finish getting that saw in place and the damage fixed. You might have to work all night to get it done before the funeral tomorrow. We all will be at the funeral.

"Right now I'm heading downtown to pick up eight new men to start to work tomorrow noon. They'll know they're on just temporarily until our injured men can get back."

Milt sat on the chair swaying from side to side.

"Damn, Milt, your face looks just awful," Helmer said, then strode out the front door.

Milt stood, weaved a bit, but made it. "Old Man is absolutely right. I made an ass of myself. Now I better get some work done or my own father might fire me."

He started for the door, missed it by three feet, and crabbed over to it and went out.

Felicia had been holding back a laugh. Once Milt

walked outside, she chuckled softly and looked at O'Grady. "I'd say you've had a good look at the real Norgard family. Dad's the practical one for planning and looking ahead. Milt can get things done, but he's emotional and gives us a lot of heart and caring. Sometimes he goes off on a wild, angry tangent, like now. Me, I just hold down the fort and count the wages into the envelopes and try to pay our bills. That's us, the Norgards."

"Your mother?"

"She died almost six years ago now. The pox. I'd heard about it, but it never worried me. Now, smallpox is one disease I'm terrified of."

"With good cause. Speaking of practical things, I better get moving if I'm going to get anything done today. I'm sorry about your people. I hope the man who lost the leg will make it."

"The doctor said Mason should pull through. He also told me you were the one who probably saved Mason's life with that tourniquet. We thank you, and I know he will. Daddy already told Mason that he still has a job with us. We'll use him on a counting job, or as a watchman, or maybe even a bookkeeper. Mason's got a wife and three small kids, and Daddy worries about them."

O'Grady stood and went over to the brown-haired girl. He picked her up in both arms, hugging her to him, and kissed her on the cheek. "Pretty lady, when I come looking for a family to be a part of, this is the first place I stop."

She turned his face and kissed him lightly on the lips. "Thank you, Canyon O'Grady. That must at least make us kissing cousins." She kissed him again, this time with more feeling, and he let her down slowly.

"That's a dangerous way to treat a mere man."

Felicia laughed and her eyes sparkled. "I already know that. Why do you suppose I risked it?"

O'Grady touched her shoulder, nodded, and walked out the front door. There was nothing else he could do.

10

O'Grady checked in at the Stillwater Home Bank. The president and only stockholder, Kirk Vuylsteke, led him into his small private office and smiled.

"Now, you were interested in United States treasury bonds. They come in one-hundred-dollar denominations. Absolutely the safest investment you can buy. Always pay interest and are as stable as the federal government."

"That's good to hear. Are any available locally?"

"Oh, my, no. I have contacts in Chicago; I order them from a brokerage house. Minneapolis doesn't really have anyone reliable enough to handle treasury bonds."

"I see. Then there isn't anyone in town who deals in them either?"

"Oh, my, no."

"Thank you. My funds haven't come in yet, but when they do, I'm thinking of some bonds. I'll let you know as soon as I can." O'Grady walked out of the bank and idled down the street.

That left only the print shop. When he'd been there before, it had looked innocent enough. Two small platen presses, but there was a back room. He couldn't do anything there until after dark. Maybe Patsy had come up with a name for Fat Charity's boyfriend. He headed that way.

A half-block behind O'Grady, Druce Gorman shifted his still-hurting arm into a more comfortable position as he trailed the tall man. So far he'd had breakfast, had gone to the mill and lost his shirt, had been back to his hotel and then back to the mill office.

Gorman had a quick dinner at the same café where O'Grady had entertained the cute little thing from the mill, then he had walked her back there and now he was on the move again.

When O'Grady went into a saloon, Gorman walked in a few minutes later, got a beer, and sat in the back. O'Grady was talking to one of the dance-hall whores. Maybe he had a thing about the ladies. He bought her a beer and they talked some more but didn't go upstairs. They talked softly so no one else could hear. Gorman finished his beer. Nothing was going to happen here. He eased past O'Grady and went outside.

He was sure the big man would be walking out soon. Gorman leaned against the Maitland General Store and waited.

Five minutes later, O'Grady came out, not looking happy at all. If O'Grady wasn't making progress, then neither was Gorman. But Gorman couldn't help the cause. He had absolutely no idea where to start looking for the counterfeiters.

He followed O'Grady back to his hotel. Gorman sat in the small restaurant across from the hotel and drank a cup of coffee as he watched the front door. If the man slipped out the alley door, he would be gone. No chance Gorman could watch both doors at once.

He decided to give O'Grady two more days. If he didn't find the counterfeiters by then, Gorman would give up the project, kill O'Grady for shooting up his arm, and return to Minneapolis, where he could work some kind of scheme. He had contacts there. He could always go back into the diploma-sales racket.

O'Grady sat in his hotel room trying to come up with some new plans. He might have to pay Charity another visit and turn on some pressure. He had an idea some realistic threats to her would bring anger and retaliation. She'd send somebody with a gun after him. O'Grady would grab the guy with the club or gun and maybe get another step up the ladder.

Patsy had been no help on who Charity was giving her ass to. That name might mean a lot. Then again it might not. As of now, he had three hours to kill before it would be dark enough to pay an unauthorized visit to Lon's Quality Printing.

He looked up as someone knocked on his door. O'Grady lifted to his feet and took three quick steps to the wall beside where the door opened. "Yeah?" he shouted.

A brutal kick from outside sent the door flying open and two shotgun blasts shattered the room. O'Grady, flat against the wall by the door, avoided all the slugs. He slammed his gun butt down on the shotgun barrel, knocking it out of the shooter's hand.

Before the gun hit the floor, O'Grady was around the door casing charging down the hall after the gunman, who was running like lightning. He saw him, a short man with a beard, gray hat, and tan shirt and pants. He took the stairs in two jumps and barged through the alley door. O'Grady held his fire to avoid hitting three guests who stared in shock.

Outside, though, Canyon got off one shot as he came out the alley door. He gained on the shooter before he made it to A Street. The man turned and snapped off a shot, but it didn't come close.

The short man tore across A Street into the alley behind the whorehouses. O'Grady was less than thirty feet behind the man when the shooter stopped suddenly, turned, and fired. O'Grady was surprised by the move, but he dived to the ground to avoid the round. He rolled to his stomach and drilled a shot at the bearded man.

His round hit the shooter in the left leg and drove him back a step. Then he darted between two whorehouses to Ohio Street. Canyon was after him and saw him turning right heading out of town.

O'Grady was panting. He was going to have to do his exercises to stay in shape. Even with the wounded leg, the attacker stretched his lead. It was another two blocks before they came to a woodsy slope that had been logged off. Now only a few hardwoods grew there around some small fir and pine. There was enough brush to get lost in.

O'Grady stopped, sighted in, and fired. His .38 didn't have that kind of range. He ran again.

Five minutes later they were in thick brush and O'Grady couldn't see his quarry. He stopped and listened. Nothing. Then a moment later he heard brush snapping and crashing ahead. O'Grady ran again.

He came to an open spot with not enough brush to hide in, and O'Grady yelled at the man when he spotted him ahead. "Who sent you to kill me? Tell me and I'll let you go."

The man laughed, sent a .45 round toward O'Grady, and ran again. O'Grady was counting. That was three shots. He had two more, maybe three.

As he ran, O'Grady kicked out the empty rounds from his weapon, loading the solid cartridges as he moved. He filled the sixth chamber and ran harder. A second wind let him gain on the bearded man. They headed down a slope and the man ahead tripped and fell, rolling twenty feet.

O'Grady was closing the gap and was now less than thirty feet from his attacker. "Don't get up or you die," O'Grady bellowed standing half behind a six-inch fir tree.

The .45 barked a shot that missed, then the man jumped up and ran. He had one round left and no way to load quickly with the cap-and-round and powder percussion system.

O'Grady saw where the man was heading and got an angle on him, running hard. He was within twenty feet before the sprinter looked back to find him. O'Grady stopped and fired. His .38 round hit the ambusher in the other leg and knocked him down. From his fallen position on the ground the man lifted the .45 to fire his last shot.

O'Grady blasted twice as fast as he could thumb

back the hammer. One round drilled through the man's right wrist and the gun spun away.

O'Grady walked up slowly, his weapon trained on the man. "Now, who the hell are you, and who hired you to shotgun me?"

"Shit! How come you didn't run out of rounds?"

"I reloaded on the run, solid cartridges. Now, who are you?"

"Sammy Sprague. Just got into town."

"So you unlimber your ten-gauge on me in my hotel room. How much they pay you?"

"A hundred."

"You work cheap, you die cheap." O'Grady lifted his .38 and the man scuttered backward on the ground.

"Hold it, hold it! You want to know who hired me?"

"If you want to say."

"It was that big fat whore, Charity. She gave me fifty and the shotgun. Said to do it and bring back the shotgun for the other fifty."

"No help, you're dead." O'Grady lifted the weapon.

"Wait, wait. I can help more. A man was leaving as I came in."

"In her private office?"

"No, her big room, her bedroom," Sammy said. "He'd just finished fucking her, from the expression he had."

"Who was he?"

"Don't know, I'm new here."

"Describe him."

"Yeah, maybe forty or forty-five. Thinning brown

hair, bald on top. He was sloppy fat, had meaty hands. Short and pudgy."

"Thanks. Could be six or eight guys in town."

"He gave her the money to pay me," Sammy went on. "I saw him. They whispered and then he gave her the fifty and left."

"Helps."

"Now, you gonna let me get to the doctor?"

"Why should I? Don't you believe in fair? You tried to kill me, now it's my turn to try to kill you. Think I'll have better luck than you did."

"No! Look, I don't know what this is all about. You can't just gun me down."

"You tried to do that to me."

"Different. Look, I'll find out who the guy is. I'll find out who he is and where he lives or works. Yeah, I can do that for you."

"Not much to be bargaining with for your life, Sammy."

"Yeah, I know, but it's all I got. You can have my Colt and that fifty dollars."

"I'll take your six-gun and gun belt. You won't need it anymore in this town. Give, now."

The man unbuckled his gun belt with his left hand and tossed it toward O'Grady.

"I'll get the weapon. You get your smelly hide in to Doc Potter and have him fix your gunshot wounds. Then you find out who the man was and tell me before seven o'clock tonight. I'll be in the alley right beside the Aces High Saloon. Don't try to ride out of town. I've got a man at the livery. Get up and get out of my sight."

O'Grady watched Sammy limp away holding his

shot-up right arm. He might find out who Charity's man was, and he might not. Either way it probably wouldn't matter.

O'Grady walked back to town, went to his hotel, had an early supper in a café he hadn't tried yet, and was in the dark alley beside the Aces High Saloon just before seven o'clock. He was forty feet into the alley looking out from the back of the saloon, using the end of the building as protection against another shotgun blast.

To his surprise a man stared into the alley, then walked down slowly. "Hey, you here? It's me, Sammy Sprague. Redhead, are you here? I ain't got a weapon. I found out."

"Back here."

Sammy walked closer. "I asked all around. Three folks told me that the guy was Carl Maitland, he owns the general store—"

O'Grady slammed the side of his .38 across Sammy's head. The bushwhacker slumped to the ground. O'Grady had seen Maitland. The man was at least six-two and looked like a child's stick figure he was so thin.

"Get out of here, Sammy. I see you again, I'll kill you for sure."

Sammy staggered up and ran down the long way of the alley, where it was pitch-black. He must have figured that was safer than the lighted street in case O'Grady started shooting.

Canyon shrugged. He'd lost on gambles before.

Ten minutes later he looked at Lon's Quality Printing office from across the street. There were no lights showing through any of the windows.

It was too early to go inside. He took a slow walk past the shop and saw windows in back and a door that led to the alley. He'd try the door first.

He went up Main, to the first café and had a cup of coffee and some cherry pie; then, with an hour wasted, he ambled back toward the print shop. O'Grady stepped into the alley when no one seemed to be watching.

At the back of the print shop, he could see no lights. When he looked at the door up close, he saw the lock was one of the latest, with pins and tumblers, and he had no idea how to break it. He looked at the windows on the off side from the alley. There was only one, low and filled with foot-square panes.

O'Grady tried to lift the double-hung sash but it was either stuck or locked. Just inside the lower pane he saw a twist lock. He found a rock in the vacant lot and held a piece of cardboard against the top of the small pane and cracked the glass with the rock.

The cardboard muffled most of the sound of breaking glass. He squatted beside the window and watched and waited. There was no reaction from inside. He saw no one rushing up from the street to discover what made the breaking-glass sound.

When he stood, he picked out chunks of glass in the small pane, pushed his hand through the void, and found the turn lock. He opened it and the window slid up easily.

O'Grady stopped and listened. After a minute he had heard nothing inside the shop, so he pushed his feet into the building, found footing, and slid the rest of his body inside.

He used matches to find a kerosene lamp; he lit it

and turned it low, at the same time shielding it with his body from the two windows as he inspected the shop. The presses were too small to print treasury bonds.

He looked under a tarp but found only a fresh stack of paper of various sizes and colors. It was laid out for a job to be done, he figured.

Ten minutes and he had the front of the shop eliminated as a possible counterfeiting location. The back room was open through a door. It had no windows, and he closed the door and turned up the lamp.

The room was no more than ten feet deep and some twenty feet wide, and contained orderly stacks of boxes of stationary paper, envelopes, and some business files. A desk was to one side. Against the other wall it was less organized, with a jumble of boxes and trash, a stack of ruined printing, empty ink bottles, and cans.

He found some brown and black ink such as was on the bonds, but he knew that every printing plant in the country probably used those colors.

The discard pile seemed large, but the man must not like to throw anything away. O'Grady took a step up on the pile at one point to examine a higher box, and the pile gave a little, then held.

Damn!

This should have been the place. Now he had to face the idea that the counterfeiter wasn't in town, that this was just an ordering spot and orders were sent to another town and another printer. Chicago, maybe? Then why bring them way out here to deliver them? Why not sell them in Chicago? It stumped him. He took one final look around, then went back to the window. He turned the lamp low and picked up all of the broken glass he could find inside the room.

What was left in the window he pushed so it fell outside. Then he dumped the glass from inside to the ground beyond the window. Now if the owner saw the window broken, he would find the glass outside and would have to assume that it had been broken from the inside.

As he got ready to leave, he stacked two empty cardboard boxes nearby. Once he had crawled through the window, he pulled the boxes over so they blocked the broken window. Then he closed it and locked it by reaching through the break.

Five minutes later he was back in his new hotel room. He had insisted that the clerk give him one that wasn't blasted with dozens of .32-caliber double-aught buck shotgun pellets. He sat on the bed with a pad and pencil trying to figure out his next move. After a half-hour, he had a page filled with squiggles and whirls.

It was no more than eight-thirty when someone knocked on his door. He jolted in three long steps to the wall beside the doorknob. He remembered the last time someone knocked on the door.

"Yeah?" he asked.

"Please, please let me in."

It was a woman's voice. He drew his .38 and cocked the hammer, then turned the key in the lock and swung the door open quickly.

Felicia Norgard stepped into the room, closed the door, and turned the key in the lock.

"I'm supposed to be at a recital at the Open

House, so I have two hours free. That should be plenty of time for us to make love." She smiled sweetly and began to unbutton the fasteners down the front of her blouse. . . .

11

"Felicia, stop it!," O'Grady ordered. He grabbed her hands. "What in the world do you think you're doing?"

"I'm taking my dress off so I can be naked and entice you to take me to bed, right here."

"Not a chance in hell, little girl," he said.

She frowned. "What do you mean? You kissed me. I thought you'd want to." She wilted.

"Of course I want to—that's just part of being a man. But I'm sure as hell not going to. You're a friend. And I promised your brother you'd be safe around me."

"I'd rather be under you." She laughed. "Isn't that naughty? I just feel like I want to make love with you. I don't care what you said to my brother. I take care of myself."

"You can feel like it all you want, just don't try doing it." He shook his head as he buttoned the fasteners on her blouse. "You just don't understand. I gave my word to your brother, and I'm not breaking it."

"Oh, pooh on your word." She reached her arms

around him and hugged him close to her. "I just want you so bad!"

He gently unfastened her hands and stepped back from her, then reached out and kissed her cheek.

"I won't go unless you really kiss me. I mean, really, like the last time. Twice. You must kiss me twice."

"Then you'll go on to the concert and be a good young lady?"

"I'm a woman, a grown woman. Yes, I'll try hard to be proper."

O'Grady bent and kissed her lips, which parted at once, and he found her tongue probing at his lips. She held the kiss a long time. When they came apart, she was breathing quickly. Her dimples popped in and her hazel eyes glistened.

"Oh, yes!" She put her hands around his neck and pulled him down and kissed his lips again. This time his mouth came open and they fought with tongues for a bit, then he retreated and she followed. She moaned as she darted her tongue into his mouth. At last she moaned again and rubbed his chest and eased away from his lips.

"Now that was a kiss," she said. She lifted her brows and watched him. "Still not enough to make you want to throw me on your bed and rip my clothes off?"

"Not quite enough."

"Guess I better go, then. I did promise. Damn!" She stamped her foot and reached for her reticule, which she had put on the dresser. "One of these days, Canyon O'Grady, after this mess is all straightened out. One of these days you and I are going to have a long talk, and then we'll make love."

She smiled sweetly at him, turned, and walked out the door as he held it open for her.

O'Grady closed the door quickly and locked it. When he saw her walk down Main Street to the Opera House, he relaxed. At least she was where she was supposed to be. He thought about the problem of finding the damn counterfeiter, and he decided maybe he'd been pushing too hard. He couldn't evaluate it all and come up with a solution. Maybe he needed some relaxation.

Ten minutes later he was in the Aces High Saloon deep into a poker game. He played at a quarter-limit table, where he couldn't win or lose much. For a while he was ten dollars ahead, then he lost half of that, and by the time he had played for two hours, he was still about seven dollars ahead. A hand had just finished when a huge man bellowed at someone who had bumped him at the bar.

"Lash," whispered one of Canyon's poker partners.

"Clumsy arse," Lash roared at the smaller man. Without waiting, he charged the man, grabbed him in his arms, and rammed him against the bar, then he let go one hand and slammed him with a fist on the jaw.

O'Grady eased back from the table.

Lash stared in surprise that his fictim still stood, and batted him again with a swinging fist that jolted the unlucky man to the floor. Janson turned and stared at the crowd of gamblers and drinkers. "He pushed me, you guys saw him."

"You're a drunken fool, Lash. Get out of the bar," O'Grady said quietly.

Lash turned until he could see O'Grady. The saloon was so qluiet the men could hear themselves breathe. "What was that?"

O'Grady stepped past a table to the cleared area near the bar. "I said, you're a drunken, clumsy oaf who ought to get the hell home, is that plain enough?"

Lash screamed and charged. O'Grady grinned, stood where he was until the last second, then stepped out of the way and slammed his heavy fist down on the back of Lash's neck as he charged past.

The big man took the blow and staggered against the bar to hold himself up. He shook his head to clear it, frowned, and at last focused on O'Grady again. "A damn fancy dan," Lash growled as he eyed O'Grady a dozen feet away.

Lash charged again, covering the distance quickly. O'Grady dodged one way, then reversed himself, but Lash had time to make only one correction and surged past where O'Grady should have been. This time O'Grady kicked the big man's foot, tripping him, and he smashed through a card table and two chairs before he rolled to the floor.

Janson got up so mad he could hardly focus on his tormentor. "Lousy bastard, you're gonna die," he screamed.

Lash didn't charge his time; he came slowly, step by step, until he was directly in front of O'Grady. The agent jabbed out two quick and hard left fists, peppering Lash's nose, bringing a gout of blood. Janson rubbed his nose with his hand, smearing blood over half his face. He roared in anger.

Lash bellowed like a gored range bull and held out both arms and rushed. O'Grady ducked under one arm and rammed his elbow into the giant's kidney as he thundered by. O'Grady spun, pounded the other kidney, then drove hard into Lash's back, grabbing him from behind and smashing him into the plank floor so hard that the bar bounced up an inch. Janson skidded on the floor and tried to roll over, but O'Grady was stretched out at an angle with his long legs spread wide. He caught one of Lash's hands and bent his thumb back toward his wrist until the thumb snapped out of joint.

Lash screeched in pain and anger.

With no warning, O'Grady jumped up and away from Lash. The giant stood slowly, holding his injured thumb and watching his enemy. His eyes were blood-red, blood covered half his face from his broken nose. He breathed through his mouth.

Lash roared again. This time he staggered forward. When he was six feet away, he stopped. O'Grady took one step forward and kicked with his right foot. Lash saw it coming but was too tired to make the quick move needed.

O'Grady's boot skidded off the huge man's inner thigh and smashed upward through his pants blasting his scrotum against his pelvic bones.

Lash stood there a second without making a sound, then he wailed and roared and sank slowly to his knees, his big hands holding his crotch protectively. He slumped to the floor and curled into a ball, sobbing and groaning with the massive pain that jolted second by second through his nervous system.

"I'll be damned," a man at the bar said. "Never seen old Lash bested by anybody before. I want to buy that redhead a drink.

He did. Half the men in the bar did. They quieted as Lash at last got to his feet; he was still bent over as he crabbed out of the saloon, his head down so he didn't have to look at anybody. When he was gone, there were more drinks, and near midnight, O'Grady decided he'd better find his hotel. He hadn't taken all the drinks offered, but he'd had almost too much. He knew he couldn't go out the front door. Lash was out there somewhere.

One of the men walked with him through the back door toward the outhouse. They went down the alley and to Main Street.

"Don't see the big fart anywhere around," the new friend told O'Grady. They hurried across the dirt street to the boardwalk on the other side and into the front door of the Lumberman's Hotel.

O'Grady got up the steps to the second floor with only a little help and prayed that there wouldn't be anyone in his room this time. He thanked the drinking buddy and sent him home.

Slowly O'Grady opened the hotel-room door. There wasn't anyone inside. He lit a match to be sure no one was there. Then he closed the door, locked it, and shoved a chair udner the knob. Gingerly he sat down on the bed and took off his boots and pants and fell into bed. Nothing would wake him until morning.

* * *

Gorman had seen O'Grady when he barged out of the hotel chasing someone that afternoon. He'd heard the shotgun blasts but didn't make the connection until later. When O'Grady came back into town and to his hotel, Gorman picked up the scent again.

O'Grady seemed to be marking time. He had coffee and a piece of pie; then, when it was fully dark, he had checked into the Lon's Quality Printing shop. Gorman could have told him he wouldn't find anything there; he himself had scouted out that place first day he hit town.

He tailed the man back to his hotel and then when he left again and went to the Aces High saloon. Gorman sat in the background during O'Grady's poker playing and witnessed the fight with Lash. It had been a work of art how the smaller man cut down Lash. Janson waited out the celebration.

Hell, he might be able to find O'Grady' drunk enough to slip a knife between his ribs as he staggered back to his hotel. O'Grady wasn't finding the bonds or the printer. But the friendly drinking buddy had ruined those plans.

Gorman watched the hotel for a while, but the condition O'Grady seemed to be in meant he must be snoring soundly by now and wouldn't be up until noon tomorrow.

Gorman stood in the shadow of the closed-up Northern Café down the block from the Lumberman's Hotel and cursed his luck. Maybe he wouldn't give O'Grady two days, after all. Maybe he should find him tomorrow and blast him full of holes and take off for Minneapolis. Yeah, maybe.

He walked down the street to the Aces High Saloon and checked out the whores. Hell, he really didn't care which one it was. He felt like pounding it off tonight. Maybe that would make him feel better.

"My name's Heather," said the dance-hall girl in the Aces High Saloon who stood beside him. "You want to drink or what?"

Gorman snorted. "First a drink and then something else? How much is a good piece of pussy worth these days?"

"Two dollars for my special customers, 'lessen you want an all-nighter. That goes for twenty."

"No woman is worth twenty dollars. I've had every kind there is."

"You ain't never had me, bucko."

"Not yet. Now bring us a couple of beers and then we'll climb them stairs over there."

They drank the beer, and before they were done, somebody outside fired three times through the small front windows. Nobody inside got hit. The apron grabbed the shotgun from behind the bar and ran outside. They heard a shotgun blast and the barkeep came back in grinning.

"That was Lash. He must still be mad about getting beat up in here tonight. He'll be madder when Doc Potter pulls that rock salt out of his butt."

The late drinking crowd laughed and Gorman grabbed Heather's hand and headed up the steps to the second floor and the cribs of perpetual pleasure.

12

Lon Cumberland arrived at his print shop just after ten o'clock that same evening. He usually waited until about this time when he had more printing to do on the bonds. No use taking any chances. He had a damn good thing going here, and he didn't want to ruin it. He made sure no one followed him, then slipped into the alley beside his store and around to the back door.

Again he looked around, then keyed the two locks on the door. One was hidden under a flap of thin wood. He let himself in and closed the door and made sure it was securely locked. Then he scratched a match, found the lamp, and lit it. There were no windows in this back room.

He went to his desk a moment, then walked to the far side, where the stack of boxes and storage items lay. Lon reached to the wall and pushed a long lever. It slowly lifted the whole mass of boxes and apparent trash. All of it was nailed and glued to a canvas-and-wood frame that swung upward against the inside wall.

Under it stood a Hildalgo press, a platen type, heavy and precise and capable of great precision printing. Nearby was a table with a cloth covering several objects.

Lon went to the table, removed the cloth, set up four kerosene lamps and lit them, then checked his work from the last printing. A dozen U.S. treasury bonds lay under the cloth. Each was now fully dry and ready for collecting and placing in an envelope. He did so, then moved to the press and carefully wiped off the engraving in the press. He checked the inker and applied more of the brown ink.

For the next hour, Lon went through the precise work of placing a piece of paper in exact registration on the press, then inking the engraving and drawing down the bar to create the needed pressure to complete the printing process. Two out of every three he printed he threw out after examining them. When he had forty printed perfectly, he laid them out on the table to dry.

Then he cleaned the brown ink off the engraving and from the press and took the main engraving out of the press. He inserted in its place another form that held the various numbers on the bond that had to be printed in black.

Now came the precise registering of the form in the press so it would meet the vacant areas left in the first printing. He tested the setup a dozen times on the discarded brown printings, and at last had it registered correctly.

Now he printed twenty of the blank pieces of paper so they showed only the numbers. Later he would add the brown printing to the bonds to complete them. Again it took him almost an hour to do the printing of the numbers, making sure each one was precisely correct and printed with the proper amount of pressure and clarity. One of every two he produced was discarded.

When he had the forty he wanted to save, he spread them on a shelf of the table to dry. Then he covered the press and relaxed with a long shot from a whiskey bottle.

A knock sounded on the back door and he frowned a moment, then remembered and hurried to the panel.

"Who is it?" he asked.

A muffled voice replied. He recognized it and undid the two locks and opened the door.

A woman stepped into the room and threw back a hood that had been covering her head.

"Patsy, you're right on time. How's my girl?"

"I'm damn good," Patsy said, one hand on a hip. "Everybody in town says I'm the best piece of ass around. What kind of wild party do you have in mind for tonight?"

"What the hell did you find out about this redhead, O'Grady?"

"Nothing you didn't already know. He's damn curious about who Charity's boyfriend is."

"You didn't tell him?"

"Hell, no. A deal is a deal. I take care of you and you take me with you when you leave town."

"About two weeks. I'll have three hundred printed by then and we can move to Chicago."

"Two weeks, you really mean that?"

"Right. I'll have my three hundred then and we'll dump the press and take the plates and head for Chicago. When I sell out on the three hundred, I'll buy another press and get back to printing."

"How much are three hundred bonds worth, to. . . . us?"

He grinned. Damn but she was hooked. "If we get fifty dollars for each one, that should be fifteen thousand dollars. Enough to live on for three or four years. Then we'll print some more."

"And I won't have to work?"

"You'll work all right. But I'll be your only customer. Twice a night at least to keep you happy."

"You still planning to kill O'Grady," Patsy said.

"Been trying. I had some men try twice. Both times they either got killed or run out of town. Even Lash has given up on the redhead. Lash got his balls kicked in tonight and then the barkeep at the Aces High peppered his ass with rock salt from a shotgun. He's through in this town. Oh, yeah, you must have been there."

"I was. You want O'Grady dead, you're gonna have to do it yourself, looks like," Patsy said. "What's so hard? He's in the hotel. He got stinking drunk tonight after beating up Lash. He should be passed out in his room by this time."

"Yeah?"

"He couldn't even walk out of the saloon without help."

Lon grinned as he buttoned up his pants. "Just maybe this is the time. You know his room?"

"He changed rooms, but I can find out. I'm a friend of the night clerk."

"Let's go."

Twenty minutes later, Lon and Patsy slipped up the back stairs at the Lumberman's Hotel.

"The clerk said O'Grady moved to Number Twenty-six."

They went up the stairs slowly so they wouldn't make any noise and down to Room 26.

Lon tried the knob and eased the door inward. "O'Grady was so drunk he forgot to lock it," he said, pushing a ring with six skeleton keys back into his pocket. He cocked the percussion .44 and eased the door open. The kerosene lamp in the hallway cast a pale-yellow oblong of light through the door as Lon Cumberland slipped quietly into the room. The light showed a man on the bed, his back toward the door, snoring softly.

A pillow lay on the floor beside the bed. Lon bent and picked up the pillow and folded it around his right hand and the weapon. Might as well muffle the sound as much as possible. He put the pillow almost against the man's broad back. Lon couldn't see the man's head in the shadows, but this had to be the man.

He pulled the trigger and the round rammed through the feather pillow into the man's back. He surged forward and started to turn. Lon cocked and fired the .44 twice more before the man could turn and Lon saw the rounds blast into the man's spinal column. Had to be dead. Nobody could live with those three rounds in his back. Lon was pleased by the hushed sound the revolver made inside the pillow. Maybe nobody in the hotel had heard it. He dropped the pillow, stamped on a tiny flame that had come from the powder burns, and backed out of the room.

"Nobody must have heard," Patsy said, looking down the hallway.

Lon pulled the door closed and the two of them walked quickly down the hall and out the back door. He hugged the woman, his eyes bright with the excitement.

"Damn! We did it!"

13

Across the hall from Room 26 in the Lumberman's Hotel, a still-fuzzy-headed Canyon O'Grady came awake suddenly. He had heard something familiar yet different. Shortly he heard it twice again, two more pops, like a muffled pistol shot. He came to his feet in Room 28 and jumped to the door.

He quietly removed the chair and unlocked the door, then he turned the knob slowly and opened the door inward just enough so he could see a slice of the hallway. His door was six feet away from the door to the room across the hallway. He stared silently at Room 26 as Lon Cumberland, the printer, came out holding a smoking revolver.

A moment later a woman joined Cumberland from in back of O'Grady's field of vision. Patsy! Now there was a team. She whispered to Lon, who had closed the door to 26, took his arm, and the pair walked quickly toward the back stairway.

O'Grady could smell the smoke and the acrid cordite in the air. Cumberland had evidently fired three times in the other room. The agent closed the door softly and locked it, and it was then that he began to sweat.

His room number was supposed to be 26. That's where all of his belongings were. How had he got in 28? He must have been too drunk last night to remember the right room. He was lucky that no one had been in this room and that the door had been left unlocked. He remembered locking it once inside and putting up the chair. Yes.

Patsy. Was she working with Cumberland? Why? It certainly moved Cumberland up as the number-one suspect if he had tried to kill O'Grady. He pondered it a minute. Yes, he was safe enough here for the rest of the night. In the morning he would decide what to do. It might be to his advantage for a short time if Cumberland thought he was dead.

As he lay back down, he wondered if there was a dead man across the hall, and if so, how he happened to be sleeping in O'Grady's bed. He knew at times night clerks were notoriously sloppy in assigning rooms. It was probably one of those mix-ups when the clerk had forgotten that he had moved O'Grady into 26 after his room had been shotgunned.

Or perhaps one clerk moved him and forgot to note it on the register or however they kept track of empty rooms. He'd find out in the morning.

O'Grady dropped back on the bed, the headache only then beginning to bother him. He hoped it would be gone by morning.

Four hours later, when he came awake, it seemed to O'Grady that he had just dropped back on the bed. He sat up in the daylight. He dressed, checked his weapon on his gun belt, slid on his low-crowned brown hat, and eased out into the hallway. It was just after six A.M. when O'Grady closed the door to 28.

He stepped to Room 26 and turned the knob. The smell was unmistakable. O'Grady didn't know the man on the bed with three blue holes in his back. He gathered up his gear and clothes and stuffed them all in his carpetbag. He put his goods in Room 28, closed and locked the door.

O'Grady continued along the hall to the far stairs and down to the alley. He had worked out his priorities. Right now he couldn't worry about the dead man back there in his former room. He had some unfinished business. He needed to find the man who called himself Rufus Thorndike. He might be back at the doctor to get his shoulder rebandaged. It would be worth a try. That would be first. The guy was about five-eight and slight, the doctor had said. He'd watch for him.

What he wasn't sure of was why Patsy had been in on the killing last night. They had been aiming at O'Grady, but why? If Lon Cumberland was, after all, the counterfeiter, O'Grady could understand the murder attempt. Which meant Cumberland had hidden everything well in his print shop.

But why was Patsy with him? Unless she was Cumberland's private special whore and had bedded O'Grady to see what she could learn from him to tell Cumberland. That could be it.

He walked down the block on Main to the Evergreen Hotel. It was at the end of the block next to Michigan Street. He found a spot across the street where he could watch the front door and slouched against the wall of the newspaper offices and waited.

By eight o'clock O'Grady decided he'd missed the false Thorndike. He walked down Minnesota Street to Dr. Potter's office. The medic was in and the door was open.

O'Grady explained his mission.

"Fact is, the man just left ten minutes ago. Said he was hungry. His shoulder isn't healing right. I treated it and bandaged it and put his arm in a sling. Told him he could wind up losing the arm if he didn't take care of it."

"Thanks. He say where he was going to eat?"

"Said he likes the Northern Café."

"What was he wearing?"

"Brown jacket, black hat, a white shirt, and no tie."

O'Grady thanked him and hurried out. His side twinged a little, but it was healing. No need to bother the doctor about it now.

The Northern Café. He thought about that as he walked toward it. Mention one place and eat at another. That would be the best tactic. He checked two small eateries before he came to the Northern, but he had seen nobody who had an arm sling or who fit Potter's description.

At the Northern Café he saw the man who said he was Thorndike sitting just inside the door at the first table. O'Grady walked in the door, sat down beside him at the table, and pushed the muzzle of his .38 against the man's side.

"We meet again, and don't tell me you're Rufus J. Thorndike. I expect you're the man who killed him in Minneapolis. Why don't we both stand up quiet like and walk out the front door? Then my revolver won't go off and blow a hole right through your worthless heart."

"Hey, I don't know you. I sure don't know what you're talking about."

O'Grady slapped the man's left shoulder and he writhed in pain.

"Guess nobody shot you in the shoulder, either. Now, on your feet so we don't make a fuss—or get you killed. Now."

They stood and walked out the door close together. O'Grady led the man down Main, across Ohio, and into the residential section of town.

"Now, tell me what this is all about. You must have followed me to town from Thorndike's place. How else would you know his name? Why did you shoot at me two or three days ago?"

"Bad idea," he said. "I shouldn't have done that."

"Who are you?"

"Name's Druce Gorman. You're right, I'm from Minneapolis. I saw you leave my friend's house and figured you killed him, so I came after you."

"No good, Gorman. You knew he was dead before I went into the place. You'll have to do better than that."

When Gorman didn't reply, O'Grady searched him and found a derringer in his jacket pocket.

"What's this for, hunting buffalo?"

"Protection. I don't like bigger guns."

"Why did you kill Thorndike?"

"I keep telling you I didn't. I knew him, we

worked together once in a while. I went to see him and saw you coming out and found him dead."

Ahead on their side of the street, a woman and four children walked toward them. There were no boardwalks here, just the dusty street with a few puddles still showing. O'Grady stepped to one side to let the woman and her brood pass. He started to nudge Gorman the same direction, but the man darted away, grabbed a three-year-old girl, and turned, using her as a shield.

"Stay back, O'Grady. I don't want to harm this little girl, but you come after me, she's gonna get hurt. You just back off and everything will be fine."

O'Grady had no chance for a shot. The margin for error was too fine, especially with the new gun he hadn't fired more than twenty or thirty times.

"Take it easy, Gorman. Nobody is chasing you. Just walk out of range and put the baby down; otherwise, I can charge you with kidnapping. That's twenty years in prison."

The woman screamed and wailed. Her other three children hugged her and the two smaller ones started to cry.

"Madam, control yourself," O'Grady said softly. "No harm will come to your child."

Gorman kept backing up, and when he was fifty feet away, he turned and ran with the small girl still in his arms. He went past the last house on the block and turned around the structure.

That was when O'Grady sprinted forward, his gun still out and the hammer back, ready.

When he got to the corner of the house and looked around, he found the small girl staring up at him.

Gorman was a block away heading down A Street and back into the business part of town. He was running.

O'Grady moved the small girl out to where her mother could see her, then ran after Gorman.

Gorman turned up the alley off A Street heading north. It was the alley behind the string of whorehouses. The man went up halfway, turned, saw O'Grady after him, and raced into the yard of the sixth house and in the back door.

Twenty seconds later, O'Grady banged open the back door and dashed in. A woman stood in the hall wearing only a petticoat. She stared at him.

"Christ, it's a main street through here today. He went upstairs."

O'Grady saw the back stairs a short way down the hall and raced for them. At the top of the stairs he was confronted with six doors opening off a hallway, three on each side. He saw no one, and heard nothing.

He shook his head. Only one way. He pushed open the first door and found a woman lying naked on the bed of the small room. She was alone.

"Anybody run in here a minute ago?" O'Grady asked.

"No, but you're welcome to stay."

He closed the door and tried the one across the hall. There he looked in on a couple in a sweating, pounding embrace. He didn't ask the question, since neither of them probably could hear him anyway.

The third door brought a giggle as he opened it. A woman sat astride a man on the bed; both were naked and lanced together.

"Look, I'm not selling tickets," the whore barked. "The other one's in the closet."

As she said it the closet door opened and Gorman stepped out, a six-gun in his hand. The hammer was not cocked. An empty gun belt hung from the bedpost.

"Down on the floor, O'Grady," Gorman said. "I got nothing to lose shooting you. You better move."

O'Grady started to bend, then he drove straight ahead, hit Gorman in the legs before he could cock the gun, and they went down in a roil of arms and legs and clothes from the closet. The whore on the bed jumped off and dumped a quart pitcher of water on them as they struggled.

Gorman slipped out of O'Grady's wet grasp and jolted out the door, leaving the six-gun behind. O'Grady had held his gun, and now he scrambled to his feet and chased the shorter man down the steps. He caught him in the parlor six feet from the front door.

O'Grady tackled Gorman. As soon as they hit the floor, he slammed his fist into Gorman's shot-up left shoulder. The man fainted dead away.

O'Grady carried Gorman down to the courthouse less than two blocks away and into the sheriff's office.

Sheriff Rex Spurlock came out of his small room and frowned.

"Who is he?" he asked.

O'Grady told him, and Gorman was escorted to one of the jail's two cells.

"Send a letter to Minneapolis on the next stage.

I'll give you a sworn deposition to the law over there. My guess is they're hunting Gorman for the murder of his former business partner Rufus Thorndike.''

14

That same afternoon, Patsy sat in Charity's bedroom, a soft smile on her face.

"Charity, I don't know why it's always so good with you. No man could ever understand. It's soft and subtle and . . . just wonderful." Patsy began to put on her clothes.

Charity's pudgy fingers stopped her. "No need for that just yet, we have plenty of time."

"We have been good for each other, Patsy, you and I. We both understand what making love is all about. You've been in town, what, for a year now?"

"Just about. It took us a while to get together." Patsy wasn't sure where this talk was going. Their session today had been fantastic, the best Patsy had ever experienced. She watched the portly woman with the huge breasts and the small dark eyes. They were hard to read.

"One thing to me is more important than any other, Patsy; that's honesty. If a person isn't honest with me, I have no sympathy at all for them. My mother taught me about loyalty and honesty when I was young.

"Sure, my ma was a whore, but she had principles

and she had good upbringing. She didn't get into the business until she was near to seventeen."

"Charity, I have to get dressed and go. I have errands I have to run today, or I don't know what I'll do."

"Soon, girl, soon. Let me have my say. I was talking about loyalty. I tell my girls here that they work for the best house on the street and they should be proud of that. If they don't think so, I ask them to move. What I really do is boot their little round asses into the alley and let them find another meal ticket.

"I met you in the little stitchery shop on First Street, wasn't that it? You came in and one of the shop-owner's best 'town lady' customers was coming, so she put the whore in the back room. I was already there getting fitted for a new gown. We hit it off that very first day, isn't that right, Patsy?"

"Yes." Patsy pulled on her pink chemise and then the soft silk underpants she had bought by mail order from a shop in Chicago.

Charity watched her start to dress, then walked, naked, to her bedroom door, turned the key, locking it, and put the key high on a shelf. "You'll stay, girl, until I'm through with my say. We were talking about loyalty and trust. I trust you and you trust me."

"Oh, Charity, there isn't anyone else. I haven't touched another girl since we first met."

"Patsy, that's not really what I'm talking about. I'm not talking about other women."

"Men?" Patsy laughed. "I have been unfaithful to you with men, I admit. Probably about six or seven a night for the past year. Surely you don't mean that."

"Little sweetheart," Charity said, walking up close to where Patsy sat. "I'm talking about Lon Cumberland. I know you've been servicing him. You knew he was my special man. How could you do that?"

Before Patsy could move, Charity reached out and grabbed one of her breasts and held it so tightly Patsy wailed in pain.

"How long you been bedding my man, Patsy?"

"Just . . . just a couple of times." Tears showed in Patsy's eyes and slipped down her cheeks.

"It was no couple of times, was it? Did you do it in the print shop?"

Patsy didn't answer.

Charity squeezed her breast and twisted.

"Yes! yes! In his shop. He said sometimes he liked a smaller woman. Honest to God, Charity, I was just a sometime thing with him."

"He said he'd take you away with him, didn't he?"

"Away? To Chicago? No! No, Charity, God help me, he never said anything about going . . . anywhere."

Charity drew back her fist and slammed it with all her weight behind it into Patsy's face. It hit her cheek, broke two bones in her face, and slammed her sideways on the fancy bed.

"Liar! Goddamned liar! Lon talks his head off whenever he's making love."

Patsy struggled to sit up. She knew something had broken in her mouth. She tasted blood. Her head hurt so she could hardly keep from screaming.

Charity went on, watching Patsy like a cobra. "Lon talks, it's just the way he is. I'm damn sure he's told you every plan he's made about the bonds and his move. How many bonds does he want to print before he goes?"

"He said three hundred . . . Oh, God!"

Charity slammed her fist into Patsy's face again, this time hitting her flush on the nose, smashing the flesh and cartilage, bringing a gush of blood. She grabbed Patsy and threw her on the floor. "Now, how long you been bedding my Lon?"

"About six months. It was his idea. Said he didn't like the saloon, so I went there."

"He pay you?"

"First two times, then I told him . . ."

Charity's face went red, almost purple. She rushed around the bedroom searching. She found the two-shot derringer a minute later under one of the satin pillows on the bed.

"Liar! Cheat! Charity held the little gun at arm's length pointing at Patsy.

Patsy stood slowly. "Charity, you can't do this. We mean too much to each other. We're alike, you and me. We know what's important."

"Damn right we do," Charity screamed. "Money, that's what's important. Lon can print and sell enough bonds so we'll have at least fifty thousand dollars. You know how much money that is, little slut? Fifty thousand dollars, more than I could spend in two lifetimes, even in New York."

Charity took a deep breath. The fury receded a little, her face lost the purple color, and she smiled.

Then she shot Patsy in the chest. Patsy jolted backward against the bed, then slid to the floor.

Charity lowered the muzzle of the little gun, put it against Patsy's forehead, and fired the second round.

She took a long breath, then began thinking how to get rid of the garbage that now cluttered her room.

15

15

Canyon O'Grady kept out of sight of the downtown area for the rest of the day. He wasn't eager for Lon Cumberland to see him—alive.

About five-thirty that afternoon, he found a hiding spot behind some barrels up the alley across from the printing shop where he could see the front door. He sat and waited. He wanted to see if Cumberland came out the door, and if so, where he went.

O'Grady tried to remember what he had told Patsy when they had spent the night together. He wasn't sure, but whatever he let slip, he was sure that Cumberland knew now. What still puzzled him was how Charity fit into the picture. He was sure Cumberland had more than a professional interest in the madam of Charity House. But if Patsy was his steady woman, where did that leave Charity? He had plenty of questions, just no answers.

Cumberland didn't figure to miss his supper, not with the weight he carried. He cooperated by coming out of his door at five-forty-five, locked it, and headed for the nearest restaurant, The High Line. Canyon found a place across the street and waited.

A half-hour later Cumberland came out picking

his teeth. He stood on the boardwalk a moment, threw the toothpick away, and walked down Main toward Minnesota, where he turned left and headed north. At A Street he turned left and went down to the alley behind whorehouse row.

O'Grady grinned and watched as the printer walked into the back door of the third house from the far end, Charity House. The agent hurried back the way he had come. He walked slowly in the alley alongside Lon's Quality Printing and looked both ways. On the other side of the building he found the same window he had broken before. The boxes were where he had stacked them and the window was still broken.

It took him only two minutes to get into the shop, then he hurried to the back room and closed the door and lit two lamps. It had to be there somewhere. He searched the desk side, but found nothing. The junk pile looked the same as before. He started moving boxes.

The third one wouldn't move. It was stuck fast. He tried another one and soon saw a pattern. The whole bottom of the "junk" pile seemed to be nailed down. Why? He stomped on it and felt the whole thing shake. It was a cover of some kind.

Near the floor he found what looked like a strip of canvas, and under that a one-by-four board. He pulled up on it and something moved on the side of the wall.

Over there a moment later he saw a long two-by-four that had ink stains on it. He grabbed it and pulled and pushed. When he pushed, the whole top of the junk pile began to lift. He pushed harder and then swung it six feet along the wall.

The cover lifted up and rested against the inner partition, revealing the printing press and the drying U.S. treasury bonds.

"Oh, yes," O'Grady said softly. When he got to the press, it took him a minute to figure out how to loosen the dogs that held the engraving in place. He lifted it out. It still had ink on it. He found a rag and wiped it off until it was clean, and put it down. Then he looked at the bonds. Some were finished, some with only one color of ink. He bunched them together in a box, kept one of the completed ones, folded it, and put it in his shirt pocket for evidence.

Then he took the rest of the bonds outside to the rear, where he had seen a burn barrel. The barrel was a fifty-gallon drum with a draft hole cut in the bottom of the side. Quickly O'Grady began feeding the sheets into the barrel, lighting each one.

Soon he had thirty or forty of the bonds burning furiously. He burned the partly done ones and a whole box of paper that had been cut into the right size for the bonds. When he had all of the bonds burned, he went back inside, picked up the plate engraving, and laid it on a marble makeup table. He found a hammer and broke the beautifully engraved plate in half.

That done, he wrapped it in a piece of paper, put it under his arm, and walked out the back door, leaving it unlocked and leaving the cover off the printing press.

O'Grady dropped off the wrapped engraving plate in his room at the hotel and headed for Charity

House. He walked in the front room, checked Charity's downstairs office, then walked upstairs toward her bedroom. Two girls yelled at him. One screeched loud enough to wake a dead man in Omaha, but O'Grady kept walking.

By the time he pushed open the door into Charity's bedroom, he found the window open and a ladder extending down to the alley behind the house.

"Sorry, you missed him," Charity said, watching O'Grady. "You really missed him."

O'Grady went down the ladder and ran down the alley. He could see Lon Cumberland in the distance, and it looked like he wore only his long underwear and had on just one shoe.

Soon O'Grady got close enough to keep sight of Cumberland easily. Lon scurried up A Street and into the first saloon he came to. O'Grady was right behind him. He saw the printer dive behind the bar and come up with the barkeep's shotgun. Cumberland didn't hesitate as he fired toward the door where O'Grady had just entered.

Canyon saw the flash of the rising weapon and dived for the floor, letting the shot slam over his head into the wooden door behind him. O'Grady rolled toward the bar. It was a barrel bar, the boards of the bartop set on six wooden barrels placed side by side.

O'Grady rolled under the bar and surged upward, taking the bartop with him and crashing it down behind the barrels. Glass and bottles shattered.

O'Grady grabbed for Cumberland, but the toppled bar kept the agent from reaching the printer. Cumberland swung at Canyon with a broken bottle, and when he dodged, O'Grady stumbled on a glass that had rolled behind him, and fell.

Cumberland darted for a door behind the bar as Canyon leapt to his feet. He raced into the room behind the bar, found only a bunk, a chair, a table, and the door half-open. Outside wasn't an alley exactly, just a pathway between the back of the buildings that fronted on A and Main streets. A thousand places to hide.

O'Grady held his breath listening. Soft footsteps sounded from the left. He followed and soon, ahead in the gloom, he saw the figure of Cumberland moving between the buildings.

"Hold it, Cumberland, or I use you for target practice."

The figure vanished for a moment and then Canyon saw a shaft of light ahead as the figure slipped into the back door of a building.

O'Grady swore softly and raced to the door. He pushed it open from the side, got no deadly response, and leapt inside. It was a kitchen. A lamp burned on a low table where several knives rested. The curtains in a draped doorway swayed gently.

O'Grady saw the flash of movement to his left and dodged away from it as a body hurtled at him, a knife held out slashing at him.

The knife missed. O'Grady stepped back as Cumberland passed by him, and brought his gun down hard on the printer's neck. Cumberland toppled to the floor. He was still conscious, though, and struggled to rise. He stopped when he felt the barrel of the gun at his neck.

"Well, the printer. Are my cards ready yet, Mr. Cumberland?"

"Bastard."

"Nothing more to say? Strange. I thought we'd have a lot to talk about, like how many of the treasury bonds you've sold so far, and where they are and how many agents you have out selling. Easy things like that."

"Go to hell. I don't know what you're talking about. You assaulted me in a public place, I ran for my life."

"Sure you did, Cumberland. I found your press. I took the plate and broke it in half and burned up all of the bonds you printed, except one for evidence."

"I still don't know what you're talking about."

"Hoped you'd say that." O'Grady bent, picked up the knife, and held it a fraction of an inch from Cumberland's eye. "Let's go out back and we'll see how much you bleed before you start remembering."

"Oh, God! Not a knife. I hate those things."

"Who else is working with you here in town?"

"Only Charity, she . . . Her place was the contact for the buyers."

"How many buyers?"

"Just one so far, from Minneapolis. Now put that damn knife down."

"What's the man's name in Minneapolis?"

"I don't know. We planned it that way. You'll have to find him on your own."

"What about Patsy?"

"I didn't kill her. Didn't have nothing to do with that. She was a good kid, I liked her."

O'Grady didn't let his surprise at the death of the young woman slow his questioning. "Who killed Patsy?"

"Damn. Charity, I think. She found out I was seeing Patsy."

"On your feet, fatty. Time we go see the sheriff."

O'Grady stashed Cumberland in the jail and turned over the treasury bond to Spurlock. He had O'Grady sign the back of the bond and date it, then the sheriff put it in his safe.

When O'Grady walked in the front door of Charity House, one of the girls ran quickly to the office curtain. The agent followed her.

Charity held a derringer aimed at his chest when O'Grady came through the drape.

"Well, the leopard finally shows her spots," O'Grady said. "The whore with a heart of gold, except the metal turns out to be fool's gold, after all."

"Not so foolish, O'Grady."

"You can put the toy away. The game is over, Charity. I just burned the bonds and broke the engraved plate. You don't have a damn thing to protect."

"You can't prove that I was involved. It isn't against the law to try to run away with a rich man."

"True. Now, put the gun down before it goes off. Some of those have damn touchy triggers."

"You didn't come here to arrest me?"

"Why would I do that? You said yourself you wanted to run away with Lon Cumberland. That's no crime."

She lowered the gun slowly, at last put it on the table beside where she sat.

"It's not a crime either if two men meet in your whorehouse and exchange money and counterfeit documents. I just wanted to be sure that you'll testify what happened here. We don't need it for the case, but it would help."

She shook her head. "No, I don't think I could testify against Lon."

"Oh, I didn't mean about Lon. I was talking about Patsy."

Faster than he thought she was capable, the fat madam lunged for the derringer. His hand got there after hers had closed around the weapon, and she stroked the trigger. O'Grady spun the derringer around, and when the hammer fell, the muzzle pointed back at Charity. The big round jolted through part of one sagging breast, sliced past a rib, and drove through her heart before it stopped.

Charity dropped the weapon and toppled sideways. She hit the desk as she fell to the floor. Her eyes flickered just once, then she was dead.

16

Canyon O'Grady woke up in Room 28 in the Lumberman's Hotel the next morning with a sense of satisfaction. Gorman and Cumberland were safely apprehended and the threat to the federal government removed. He dressed, broke his fast, and headed for the Norgard mill.

Felicia met him at the office door. She wore an attractive dress that made it plain she was a woman. Her soft brown hair had been brushed at least a hundred times that morning, and it hung around her shoulders like brown mist. Her hazel eyes watched him. "I heard you solved the crime about those counterfeit bonds. Now you're free for a picnic this noon. I'll go home at eleven and expect you to pick me up there at twelve sharp."

"I'll be glad to come on an afternoon picnic. How goes the lumber war?"

"Oh, that. It's all over. In fact, Daddy and two of the Rombolds are talking about some kind of a joint rafting operation to get the logs down the river quicker and with fewer lost logs. We've all agreed to keep Milt and Roman under control."

Helmer came out of his office. "Thought I heard

a familiar voice out here." He walked forward holding out his hand. "Want to thank you again for helping us get this little problem of ours straightened out. Looks like things are going to be on an even keel now. Milt is still stewing, but he'll get over it."

O'Grady stayed for half an hour, talking with the two of them, then said he had some chores to finish up before noon. He walked back to the barrel bar he had smashed up trying to get at Cumberland and settled up with the owner for the damages.

O'Grady paid the man from his wallet and walked down the street to Dr. Potter's office.

"One more chance to check my side where I got in the way of that hot lead, Doc." O'Grady said.

The tall medic told O'Grady to take off his shirt and then checked the wound. The bandage had slipped half off and one part of the wound had broken open where it had started to heal.

"You been fighting off the whole north woods, boy?" Dr. Potter asked. He put on some salve and rebandaged it. "Should hold you until your next fistfight."

O'Grady gave him a dollar and headed for the Norgard house down on Minnesota Street. If he walked slowly, he'd still be half an hour early.

When O'Grady rang the bell at the front door, Felicia swung the big door wide.

"Good, you're early. You can help me hitch up Polly. I never did understand where all those straps and rings and things go."

"What's for our picnic dinner?"

"You don't get to peek until we drive out there,"

Felicia said, laughing. "You might decide not to come."

"Not a chance! I need an afternoon to sit in the sun and rest and relax. Any fish in that river?"

"Plenty, but we're not taking fishing poles."

They loaded the picnic basket in the buggy and he helped her up to the seat. A length of shapely leg showed and she watched to see if he noticed. He did, but he didn't say anything.

"Let me drive," she said like an eager schoolgirl. "I love to drive, but Daddy will never let me, says it isn't ladylike."

They took the river road off Minnesota Street, which followed the river except on its more serious twists and turns. About half a mile out of town downstream, Felicia turned the rig off the dirt road into a grove of trees and along a faint track to the edge of the river.

The spot was behind enough trees so the buggy couldn't be seen from the road.

"This is the spot, isn't it marvelous? We can spread a blanket right over there and be able to see the river and everything."

When the blanket was down, the picnic basket anchoring one corner of it, Felicia sat down in the middle of the blanket and crooked her finger at him. "I have a favor to ask," she said primly.

"A favor? What?"

She patted the spot beside her and he sat down; she put her arms around his neck and pulled his face to her and kissed him. It was a hot, passionate kiss, and O'Grady enjoyed it a moment, then eased away.

"That's just the start of the favor," Felicia said.

She took his hand and pressed it against her breasts. "You're not slipping away this time, Canyon O'Grady." She pointed a finger at him. "And don't say a word about promises made to Milton. I'm a big girl and I can take care of myself, and right now I want to take care of you."

She kissed him again and then eased backward and pulled him down gently with her so he lay half on top of her on the blanket.

"Now, don't you think this is a good idea? We both can just relax and appreciate each other for a while."

"Felicia . . ."

She kissed his lips gently to stop the words. "You don't have to tussle with your conscience, Canyon. I'm not a virgin. There, I said it. You won't be stealing my virginity." She opened the buttons on the dress and he saw there was nothing under it. His hand closed over one of her breasts and she moaned softly and sighed.

"Now, Canyon O'Grady, show me what an expert kisser you are, and build my fires so hot I want to explode."

He stroked the creamy white skin of her breast and then the pinkness of her areola. Gently he reached in and kissed her pink bud of a nipple. Her hips moved against his once, then he kissed her nipple again and bit it and sucked half her breast into his mouth.

"Oh, sweet Lord," she whispered, and she moaned in delight. "Now take off my clothes. I want to be all naked and bare and let you play with me as I undress you."

As soon as he had her cotton drawers pulled down, Felicia pushed her hand inside his pants and found his swollen member. She held it gently as he pulled off the rest of his clothes.

Felicia sat up, her hand-size breasts bouncing, her eyes alive and eager. She touched the red hair on his chest, then worked on his boots and at last took down his pants and short underwear. "Such a monster," she breathed softly, and held him and stroked him gently, kissing him. Then she moved over, lying on top of him, covering him, pressing her breasts into his chest and her hips working a slow grinding on his hardness.

His hands worked down her torso and she gasped when he found her crotch.

"Please touch me, rub me, it feels so good."

He did as she asked, then she turned over and pulled him with her.

"Right now, Canyon, right now."

He entered her and eased forward and she shouted in joy, then erupted into gasping and moans, her arms tight around his back as he slid all the way in her soft, steamy slot and they were spiked together.

"Oh, yes, what I dreamed of," Felicia crooned. "Only so much, much better. I'm glad you waited; it makes it sweeter." Then her eyes lit up like sparklers on a dark night. "Now, O'Grady, right now! All the way. I can't stand it."

He worked gently with her, but her hips pounded up hard to meet him and she tugged and worked on him inside on every stroke. Soon he was building and building, and not sure he could stop.

"If you stop now, O'Grady I'll strangle you," Felicia hissed.

They pounded a dozen more times, then he let it explode and shattered himself, vaporizing and floating in the heavens, weaving in and out of the stars, jolting six times into her eager body; then he eased down on her and she finished her own climax.

Ten minutes later they slipped into their clothes, but she left her blouse unbuttoned to tease him. She pulled the picnic basket over and they explored it.

Fried chicken, potato salad, fresh-baked bread, sliced tomatoes, a container of coffee that was still warm, if not hot, and three kinds of dessert. They ate until they were stuffed.

"I want to wade in the water," she said.

He followed her, rolled up his pants legs, and waded, finding some tiny fish darting around. Back on the blanket they let their feet and legs dry in the sun of the warm afternoon.

"Nice, huh?" Felicia said.

"Nice, extremely nice. But you know it can't last. I'm going to be leaving on the noon stage tomorrow."

"Oh, no! Not so soon. Then you can come to the house tonight and we can make love in a real bed and—"

He held up his hands. "Let's just concentrate on right now."

They stretched out on the blanket and made love again, slowly, deliciously.

"Better than the first time," she said as they lay in the speckled sunshine coming through the trees.

"Gets better and better." She looked at him, gently kissed his lips.

They lay in each other's arms and O'Grady was thinking downstream. Tomorrow morning he would make final arrangements for taking the prisoners to Minneapolis. Then there would be a day or two with the federal judge there getting the charges filed and his own testimony given, and the bonds and the engraving entered into evidence.

Then he would wire General Wheeler at the White House that his mission there was done, and he'd be told to come back to Washington or sent on another task.

Canyon O'Grady looked up through the leaves, felt the excited, lovely woman beside him, and gently stroked her breast.

Yes, this was the way to live. Even as he thought it, he wondered where he would be next week, tried to guess what his new assignment would be.

KEEP A LOOKOUT!

**The following is the opening section from the third novel in the action-packed new Signet Western series
CANYON O'GRADY.**

CANYON O'GRADY #10
THE GREAT LAND SWINDLE

*August, 1860, New Mexico Territory . . .
in the face of greed and ambition,
old loyalties mean nothing, human life
is cheap, and a good friend is
more precious than gold.*

Canyon O'Grady sat on the black mare and looked across the last little rise outside Santa Fe. The air was so clear that the little town cradled between the four mountain ranges had the look of an early Spanish painting.

He lifted his wide-brimmed gray hat and wiped sweat from his forehead. Even at an altitude of more than seven thousand feet the air was hot and dry this August afternoon. Canyon was letting the mare rest as much as he was allowing himself a pause. She had been working hard the last three miles and he was in no big rush. His work was done twenty miles to the west. He had to make one last stop in Santa

Excerpt from THE GREAT LAND SWINDLE

Fe before buying a ticket on the east-bound stage and heading out on the Santa Fe trail for St. Louis and then on to the long ride back to Washington D.C.

He liked the smell of the ponderosa pines that covered this far end of the great Rocky Mountain range. He took a deep breath and nudged the black down the trail. He should be in Santa Fe well before dark.

It was only a little after five o'clock when he tied his black outside *La Conchita,* the best restaurant in the old Spanish section of Santa Fe. He slapped his hat on his pants and shirt to get off some of the trail dust. He had taken a room at the hotel nearby and now went inside the café and found a table.

Here you didn't order, a waiter brought salsa and broken tortillas and a big mug of beer. Later he served Canyon a huge plate filled with refried beans and half a dozen rolled tortillas stuffed with meat, hot peppers, and cheese.

He had almost finished his meal when he saw a man at an adjoining table watching him. Canyon's right hand relaxed and dropped near his right thigh to be close to the tied down Colt .45 that rested there in leather.

Canyon watched the stranger a moment and the man grinned and stood. He came directly toward Canyon's table. The tall man eased to his feet, his gun hand still close to iron.

"I'll be a son-of-a-bitch," the stranger said, "If you ain't Canyon O'Grady you're sure his twin brother."

Excerpt from THE GREAT LAND SWINDLE

Canyon tensed more. The man was smiling, But he remembered an outlaw in Wyoming who always smiled grandly when he killed someone.

The man stopped four feet from Canyon, his grin broader now. "Damn, got to be Canyon O'Grady, with that red hair and that ugly face, who else could it be?" The man paused. He was four inches under six feet, broad-shouldered, and looked fit, but had a white face of a man not out in the weather or wind much. His hands were clean, and so were his fingernails. He was slender, well-dressed, and had a sturdy moustache squared off on the ends. The man chuckled. "You still don't remember me, do you, Canyon?"

The stranger lifted one hand and grinned. "Hey, relax, I'm friendly. I'm not gunning for you. Ease up there, old man. I knew you when we both were snot-nosed kids, about ten or twelve-years-old. Remember Almont Street in Brooklyn?"

Canyon looked at this man closer now, memories flooding back.

"Paddy?" Canyon asked.

"Damn, you do remember. Yeah. Paddy McNamara. Rooster McNamara's oldest. We lived two houses down from you on the same side of the street."

"I'll be damned!" Canyon said. He held out his hand and the other man shook it. "Don't think I would have recognized you, Paddy, if you hadn't mentioned Almont Street. Hell, you're twice as ugly as you were then."

They both laughed.

Excerpt from THE GREAT LAND SWINDLE

"Sit down," Canyon said. "Finished your supper?"

"Just did. What the hell you doing in a down-in-the-mouth place like Santa Fe, Canyon?"

"Passing through, mostly. Planning on grabbing the stage in a day or two and heading out for St. Louis."

Paddy McNamara motioned with one of his hands.

"You all finished eating?"

"Enough, I guess."

"Good, let's find a saloon and I'll buy you a couple of drinks. I got an idea to hit you with."

"What sort?"

"Not worth mentioning until we have at least three beers."

They went to the first saloon down the boardwalk, ordered, and took the frothy mugs to a table near the wall. For half an hour they remembered the trouble they had gotten into as two kids in Brooklyn.

They had downed four beers each when Paddy bought a bottle of whiskey and brought two glasses to the table. They worked on the whiskey for a while, Paddy drinking twice what Canyon did. At last Paddy got around to his news.

"Canyon, old friend, in three days I got a little job to do for a friend. All I have to do is meet the stage coming down the trail from Albuquerque and stop it about five miles south of town. I'm looking for a few men to help me do it."

"Stop the stage?" Canyon repeated. "What for?"

Excerpt from THE GREAT LAND SWINDLE

"Didn't ask. When some slick gent offers me two hundred dollars in gold just to stop a stage, hell, it's gonna get stopped. The stage from the south gets into town about four in the afternoon. So we stop it about three. Ain't quite figured out how, yet."

Canyon stared at his years-ago-best-friend. He'd had a few drinks, but he wasn't so drunk that he'd forgotten that stopping a stage with mail on board was a federal crime. A man could get a year in jail for doing that.

"You ain't gonna rob the strong box, are you?" Canyon asked.

"Hell no! Not with just a couple of men and not five miles from town. I might be dumb, but I'm not that stupid. Don't know why Arch wants the stage stopped. He just said to stop the damn thing. So, hell, we'll stop it, then we all run like sons-of-bitches."

"Sounds fishy as hell," Canyon said. "Whole thing sounds fishy as all get out. Why does somebody want to stop the stage so close in? Did this Arch say why?"

Paddy drained the last of the whiskey in his glass. "He didn't. Said it was none of my damned business. Bet if we get him drunk, he'd tell us. Let's go find him."

Canyon thought for a moment about tracking this Arch down. But he'd had more to drink than he should have in order to handle a confrontation well. And Paddy was too drunk to be relied on.

Excerpt from THE GREAT LAND SWINDLE

"No, no, not me." he responded. "I'm too damn tired. Going to get some sleep."

Paddy stared at his old friend, then nodded. "That's a good idea. You're drunk."

Canyon just smiled and stood up. It took three tries to get Paddy to his feet.

"What's the name of your hotel?"

Paddy stared at him and shook his head. "Huh? Damned if I know. Near the restaurant."

Canyon helped Paddy out of the saloon and along the boardwalk to the eatery.

At the third hotel they tried the room clerk grinned at them and said Paddy was in room 12. Canyon helped him up the stairs and down the hall to his room.

"I'll see you tomorrow, old friend," Paddy said. "Got to convince you to help me."

Canyon returned to his own room, and without taking off his shirt or even his boots, he smashed into sleep and didn't wake up until well past dawn the next morning.

The room was light but it took Canyon five minutes to realize that he was alive. He had mixed too much booze last night. Paddy McNamara. I'll be damned. Hadn't even thought of the short, tough little kid for ten years. They used to be best friends, got in and out of more trouble than you could shake a stick at. Kids. Damn, but those were fun days.

Canyon sat up at last and tried to still the pounding in his head. He grinned thinking about how Paddy must feel. A good hot cup of coffee usually ruined a hangover. He washed, dressed, brushed off his hat,

Excerpt from THE GREAT LAND SWINDLE

and headed down to the street. Half a block down he saw a sign that said "Breakfast 25 cents". He walked in and sat down.

"Eggs or flap jacks?" a voice asked him. He looked up to find a smiling pretty girl with a stub pencil poised over a pad of paper. She had the biggest brown eyes he had ever seen set in a cute round face and framed by jet black hair. She grinned at him.

"Three eggs sunnyside up, two flap jacks and a batch of country-fried potatoes, toast and coffee," Canyon said.

The girl hesitated, staring directly into his eyes for a moment. Then she smiled and turned away. Her full breasts swung against the thin blouse and at last decided to go with her.

By the time the breakfast came Canyon had reviewed his conversation with Paddy. Paddy had been hired by Arch somebody to stop the stage. Why stop a stagecoach outside the town? The most obvious answer was to rob it. But Paddy wasn't a robber, or so he said. Why else? Kidnap someone? Kill a passenger? He thought it through as he finished his breakfast. He needed to talk to the sheriff. Without knowing who this Arch might be, Canyon couldn't even try to anticipate his motives.

He went up to the counter, paid his quarter for the meal and gave the waitress a dime tip. That brought him a large smile.

Canyon found the sheriff's office after a short search and sat down to talk with Luke Parrish, sheriff of Santa Fe County.

Excerpt from THE GREAT LAND SWINDLE

Briefly, Canyon laid out his chance meeting with his old friend and the proposition he had offered.

"An interesting situation," the sheriff replied. "Why are you so damn concerned?"

Canyon took out his wallet and showed him a thin card on which was glued a small tintype photo of Canyon. The card said that Canyon O'Grady was a Special Agent of the U.S. Government on assignment by President James Buchanan. "All cooperation is expected by local, county and state law enforcement agencies and officials." The card was signed by President Buchanan.

Sheriff Parrish read the card, checked the picture against Canyon and handed it back. "Well now. I've never seen one of those cards before. Must not be many of you. I can see why you were concerned."

"Stopping a stage coach carrying U.S. mail is a federal offense. And almost all stages carry mail these days. But first I need to ask, who is this Arch?"

"That could be a problem. The first man I can think of is Archibald Forester, one of our local politicians. He's ambitious and not beyond stretching the law a bit here and there for his own benefit. He's one of the most powerful men in the territory."

The sheriff snapped his fingers. "Three days from yesterday makes it the fourteenth. I had a letter here somewhere about the fourteenth. Where was it?" He looked around his desk a minute, then grabbed a sheet of paper.

Excerpt from *THE GREAT LAND SWINDLE*

"Yeah. On the fourteenth, we're having some visitors. I'm supposed to be sure to present some security at the stage depot for the four P.M. arrival of our territorial governor, along with the junior United States senator from Iowa."

"So important people are arriving and Archibald Forester wants the stage stopped outside of town? Sounds ominous to me, Sheriff."

"Damn ominous." Parrish lit a pipe he'd been tamping full of tobacco. "You're on assignment right now, Canyon?"

"Just finished one. I was going to head east this afternoon. But now I might stay around a while. Help you find out what's going on. I could send a letter to my office and tell them I'm needed here for a while. I might be able to help out."

"Well, if you have the time. If Archibald Forester is mixed up in this I could use some help."

Canyon asked the sheriff to telegraph General Wheeler that he would be delayed. Parrish agreed, and with that settled, he walked out the front door. And almost collided with Paddy McNamara.

"Canyon! You double-crossing son-of-a-bitch! What the hell were you doing talking to Parrish?"

McNamara backed up slowly, his right hand hovering over a six-gun on his hip that Canyon saw was tied down low.

"You told the sheriff everything, didn't you, O'Grady? What kind of a back-stabber have you turned into? It doesn't matter none, because in about ten seconds you're gonna be dead."

Canyon knew there was nothing else he could do.

Excerpt from THE GREAT LAND SWINDLE

He saw the other man's hand dart upward hitting the butt of his revolver, starting its upward movement. With a touch of sadness and regret, Canyon reached for the deadly .45 six-gun in his holster.

① SIGNET (0451)

RIDING THE WESTERN TRAIL

- [ ] **THE TRAILSMAN #99: CAMP SAINT LUCIFER by Jon Sharpe.** Skye Fargo blazes away against an infernal killing crew as he follows a terror trail of corpses to a secret encampment where men kill like savages. (164431—$3.50)

- [ ] **THE TRAILSMAN #100: RIVERBOAT GOLD by Jon Sharpe.** Skye Fargo steers a deathship through a rising tide of terror on the evil end of the Mississippi. (164814—$3.95)

- [ ] **THE TRAILSMAN 101: SHOSHONI SPIRITS by Jon Sharpe.** Sky Fargo blazes through a maze of redskin magic and savage murder to aid a beautiful woman who leads him over the Rockies to a lot of trouble. (165489—$3.50)

- [ ] **THE TRAILSMAN #102: CORONADO KILLERS by Jon Sharpe.** Skye Fargo wages a one-man war against a maddog gang and an army of evil in the Southwest. With more targets than he can tick off in his gunsights, it's the firefight of his life! (165837—$3.50)

Buy them at your local bookstore or use coupon on next page for ordering.

⊘ SIGNET (0451)

UNTAMED ACTION ON THE WESTERN FRONTIER

☐ **THE TERREL BRAND by E.Z. Woods.** Owen Terrel came back from the Civil War looking for peace. He and his brother carved out a cattle kingdon in West Texas, but then a beautiful woman in danger arrived, thrusting Owen into a war against an army of bloodthirsty outlaws. He would need every bullet he had to cut them down.... (158113—$3.50)

☐ **CONFESSIONS OF JOHNNY RINGO by Geoff Aggeler.** It was a showdown for a legend: Johnny Ringo. Men spoke his name in the same hushed breath as Jesse and Frank James, the Youngers, Billy the Kid. But those other legendary outlaws were gone. Only he was left, and on his trail was the most deadly lawman in the West. (159888—$4.50)

☐ **SALT LAKE CITY by A.R. Riefe.** Mormon settlers and U.S. soldiers are on the brink of catastrophic conflict—in a Western epic of challenge and triumph. (163265—$4.50)

☐ **A LAND REMEMBERED by Patrick D. Smith.** Tobias MacIvey started with a gun, a whip, a horse and a dream of taming a wilderness that gave no quarter to the weak. He was the first of an unforgettable family who rose to fortune from the blazing guns of the Civil War, to the glitter and greed of the Florida Gold Coast today. (158970—$4.95)

☐ **THE HOMESMAN by Glendon Swarthout.** A spinster, an army deserter, and four women who have gone out of their minds and out of control on a trek through the wildest west that turns into the ultimate test for them all. A Spur Award winner. "As good as novels get."—Cleveland Plain Dealer. (164296—$4.95)

Prices slightly higher in Canada

Buy them at your local bookstore or use this convenient coupon for ordering.

NEW AMERICAN LIBRARY
P.O. Box 999, Bergenfield, New Jersey 07621

Please send me the books I have checked above. I am enclosing $_____
(please add $1.00 to this order to cover postage and handling). Send check or money order—no cash or C.O.D.'s. Prices and numbers are subject to change without notice.

Name_____

Address_____

City _____ State _____ Zip Code _____

Allow 4-6 weeks for delivery.
This offer is subject to withdrawal without notice.

ⓈSIGNET (0451)

MATT BRAUN'S BRANNOCKS SAGAS

☐ **THE BRANNOCKS.** They are three brothers and their women—in a passionate, action-filled sage that sweeps over the vastness of the American West and shines with the spirit of the men and women who had the daring and heart to risk all to conquer a wild frontier land.
(143442—$3.50)

☐ **WINDWARD WEST: THE BRANNOCKS #2.** Divided dreams pit brother against brother ... each going his own way ... until the paths cross and their conflicts explode. This is their saga as they follow their dreams through the American western frontier, where only the strongest survived.
(147014—$3.50)

☐ **RIO HONDO: THE BRANNOCKS #3.** The Brannock clan squares off against cattle rustlers and crooked politicians in this saga of the western frontier. The Brannocks pay a heavy price of blood and tears in their attempt to clean up the New Mexico territory for a new generation full of promise and glory....
(149556—$3.50)

☐ **A DISTANT LAND: BRANNOCKS #4.** The violent and passionate saga of the Brannocks continues. Ties of blood bound them together. But in a New Mexico territory where two kinds of people and two ways of life moved inexorably towards a savage showdown, unbending Brannock pride and iron Brannock will threatened to rip them apart....
(150988—$3.50)

Buy them at your local

bookstore or use coupon

on next page for ordering.

ⓢ SIGNET (0451)

SWEEPING SAGAS FROM MATT BRAUN

- [ ] **JURY OF SIX by Matt Braun.** Luke Starbuck, gun in hand, is out to deliver justice to a killer who laughs at the law—an old Western hero and outlaw who won't be tamed—Billy the Kid. (166655—$3.95)

- [ ] **EL PASO by Matt Braun.** El Paso was the wildest town in untamed Texas after the Civil War. Here men came with dreams of empire, and women with hopes of a better life on a virgin frontier. But Dallas Stoudenmire came to El Paso for a different reason—to end the reign of terror of the two vicious Banning brothers. In a town where his first mistake would be his last, Dallas was walking a tightrope.... (158430—3.50)

- [ ] **BUCK COLTER by Matt Braun.** Ruthless rancher Colonel John Covington wasn't about to let Buck Colter put down stakes and graze his herd on the open range he hogged for himself. But Colter had ideas of his own—mainly a blood score to settle with Covington. (161556—3.50)

- [ ] **CIMARRON JORDAN by Matt Braun.** No man could match Cimarron Jordan's daring and only one could match his gun ... as he followed the thunder of buffalo, the roar of rifles, and the war cries of savage Indian tribes across the great Western Plains. (160126—$3.95)

Buy them at your local bookstore or use this convenient coupon for ordering.

NEW AMERICAN LIBRARY
P.O. Box 999, Bergenfield, New Jersey 07621

Please send me the books I have checked above. I am enclosing $_____
(please add $1.00 to this order to cover postage and handling). Send check or money order—no cash or C.O.D.'s. Prices and numbers are subject to change without notice.

Name_____

Address_____

City _____ State _____ Zip Code _____

Allow 4-6 weeks for delivery.
This offer is subject to withdrawal without notice.